It is the height of the Roaring Twenties – a fresh enthusiasm for the arts, science, and exploration of the past have opened doors to a wider world, and beyond...

And yet, a dark shadow grows over the town of Arkham. Alien entities known as Ancient Ones lurk in the emptiness beyond space and time, writhing at the thresholds between worlds.

Occult rituals must be stopped and alien creatures destroyed before the Ancient Ones make our world their ruined dominion.

Only a handful of brave souls with inquisitive minds and the will to act stand against the horrors threatening to tear this world apart.

Will they prevail?

ALSO AVAILABLE IN ARKHAM HORROR

THE DROWNED CITY

The Forbidden Visions of Lucius Galloway by Carrie Harris
The Nightmare Quest of April May by Rosemary Jones

THE ADVENTURES OF ALESSANDRA ZORZI

Wrath of N'kai by Josh Reynolds
Shadows of Pnath by Josh Reynolds
Song of Carcosa by Josh Reynolds

THE FIZTMAURICE LEGACY

Mask of Silver by Rosemary Jones
The Deadly Grimoire by Rosemary Jones
The Bootlegger's Dance by Rosemary Jones

In the Coils of the Labyrinth by David Annandale

Litany of Dreams by Ari Marmell

The Ravening Deep by Tim Pratt
Herald of Ruin by Tim Pratt

The Last Ritual by S A Sidor
Cult of the Spider Queen by S A Sidor
Lair of the Crystal Fang by S A Sidor

The Devourer Below edited by Charlotte Llewelyn-Wells
Secrets in Scarlet edited by Charlotte Llewelyn-Wells

Dark Origins: The Collected Novellas Vol 1
Grim Investigations: The Collected Novellas Vol 2

ARKHAM HORROR INVESTIGATORS GAMEBOOKS

The Darkness Over Arkham by Jonathan Green

Welcome to Arkham: An Illustrated Guide for Visitors
Arkham Horror: The Poster Book

The Tides of Innsmouth

Jonathan Green

First published by Aconyte Books in 2025
ISBN 978 1 83908 335 8
Ebook ISBN 978 1 83908 336 5

Technical assistance by Victor Cheng

Cover art by Joshua Cairós • Book design by Nick Tyler

Interior art by Ryan Barger, Joshua Cairós, Matthew Cowdery, Alexandre Honore, Tomasz Jedruszek, Alexander Karcz, Marc Molnar, Pixoloid Studios & Magali Villeneuve

Printed in the United States of America and elsewhere.
9 8 7 6 5 4 3 2 1

ACONYTE BOOKS
An imprint of Asmodee North America
Mercury House, North Gate,
Nottingham NG7 7FN, UK
aconytebooks.com

For Victor Cheng.

Greetings Investigator.

Welcome to Innsmouth.

By entering the pages of this Investigators Gamebook, you have taken on the role of one of the brave Investigators driven to get to the bottom of a mystery lurking in the half-drowned fishing port of Innsmouth.

If this is your first Investigators Gamebook, read on. If you've previously played one or more Investigators Gamebooks, turn to page **282** and read the section entitled "Continuing the Adventure" before you begin this gamebook.

A gamebook is both a book and a game. The choices you make – as well as your success in tests of **WILLPOWER**, **INTELLECT**, and **COMBAT** – will determine the route you travel through the book, deciding victory or defeat in your attempts to unravel the unfolding mystery within. If you've played other adventure gamebooks outside of the Investigators Gamebooks, you'll be familiar with the concept, but this is Innsmouth, and a few things are a little… different. So, you'll want to read over the next couple of pages before your investigation begins.

Unlike most other kinds of games, you don't need to learn the rules before you start to play, but you should embrace what it means to be an Investigator to the fullest. Take note of names, locations, and anything else that might prove advantageous to you on your adventure. Some clues are obvious while others are obscure. If you're new to this type of adventure, or simply eager to begin, you have the choice to bypass some of the following instructions and leap right in. The book presents the choices you will be required to make and the tests that you will face as you go along. However, if you're curious to understand the further complexities, there are just a few things you will need before you start and additional pointers it will prove useful to know.

WHAT YOU WILL NEED

You will need some ordinary six-sided dice – a couple is plenty. Grab them now... good work. You will also need something to keep track of your Investigator's progress. You can use the character sheet on page **284**, or a notepad, or piece of paper. You can also download character sheets from our website, *https://aconytebooks.com/aconyte-extra*. You'll need something to write with, and as your Investigator can both acquire and lose **CLUES**, **RESOURCES**, **HEALTH**, **SANITY**, **[ITEMS]** and **{ABILITIES}** over the course of their investigation, a pencil is ideal. Most importantly, you'll need to choose the Investigator whose role you will be playing once you begin the adventure.

CHOOSING AN INVESTIGATOR

You can find Investigator profiles for three Investigators on page **14-17**: the sailor Silas Marsh, the folklorist Kōhaku Narukami, or the trawler Marion Tavares. Each Investigator's profile shows all their skills, **{ABILITIES}**, **{WEAKNESSES}** and **[ITEMS]**, as well as their starting **HEALTH** and **SANITY**. Before you begin, you should copy these over to your character sheet – or simply download the pre-filled version of the character sheet for your chosen Investigator from our website.

There are more Investigators you'll find as downloadable characters on our website, but if this is your first time playing through an Investigators Gamebook, we recommend using one of the three Investigators that come with this book first. Each of the Investigators featured in this gamebook has a unique introduction, which will also tell you where to begin your adventure. However, if you choose to play as a character from a different Investigators Gamebook, or a character downloaded from the Aconyte Books website, you will need to start your adventure at Entry **1**. As a reminder, if you've already successfully completed an Investigators Gamebook, make sure to review the section on page **282** that tells you how to continue the adventure with your chosen Investigator.

CHARACTER SHEETS

Now that you have your character sheet, you are ready to begin, but first it's useful to know a little more about the information your character sheet presents. Your character sheet represents you in the role of your chosen Investigator. You are them now, and their fate is your fate. The character sheet tracks your progress through a number of game stats, and also provides space to record anything you pick up along the way, such as **CLUES** and **RESOURCES**.

SKILLS: WILLPOWER, INTELLECT, AND COMBAT

Each investigator has three skills: **WILLPOWER**, **INTELLECT** and **COMBAT**. Throughout the adventure, you'll face challenges which test these skills in many different ways. When facing one of these tests, the entry in question will explain how to resolve it. Skills are represented by a number, and this number may occasionally change during the investigation.

HEALTH AND SANITY

These two game stats describe your Investigator's current physical and mental well-being. Like skills, they are represented by a number and tend to go down as the adventure goes on – in fact, they can even go negative, although they can also go up. A lower **HEALTH** or **SANITY** score will negatively impact your chances when faced with various challenges. Once these stats dip below zero, however, things will be continuously affected, and we urge you to reference your character sheet to account for those impacts. Try not to lose your mind, if you please.

ABILITIES AND WEAKNESSES

Abilities and Weaknesses represent special aptitudes or limitations peculiar to your chosen Investigator. Most Investigators start with a small number of each, and you may acquire other types of Abilities and Weaknesses as your investigation progresses. These Abilities and Weaknesses are represented by keywords, which don't do anything in and of themselves, but which may trigger bonuses or penalties, or other effects, depending on the challenges you encounter during the adventure. You don't need to memorize your Investigator's Abilities and Weaknesses. Instead, when an entry mentions an Ability or Weakness, you should check on your character sheet to see whether or not the effects described apply to you.

Sometimes, however, you may gain an Ability or Weakness as your investigation progresses. The mysteries surrounding Innsmouth are not for the faint of heart and can rattle any hardened Investigator, gifting you with proclivities such as **{HAUNTED}** or **{PARANOID}** that don't simply fade away. Yet, great powers and abilities can also be obtained… if one has the fortitude and cleverness to earn them. These too, for good or for ill, do not simply disappear.

Most Investigators also start with a Major Ability and a Major Weakness. You can only ever have one of each of these, and you can't lose or gain them during the course of an adventure. These Major Abilities and Major Weaknesses represent key aspects of your Investigator's personality, and each gives you a special rule, which makes playing the adventure unique to you and your character. They are detailed on your Investigator profile.

DOOM

The deepening mysteries and their consequences impact not just you, but the world around you. As Innsmouth steadily succumbs to the eldritch mysteries that threaten to claim the town, the state of the environment shifts accordingly. **DOOM** will appear as you further unravel the mystery contained within, representing a worsening state for humanity, but a more favorable one for the creatures and Ancient Ones influencing the town. Obtaining **DOOM** is most inadvisable. Try not to hand the universe over to the eldritch beings, won't you?

ITEMS

Items are exactly what you would expect: various objects your Investigator might carry with them or pick up along the way. For example, right now you have your [**PENCIL**] and your [**SIX-SIDED DICE**]. These items are keywords without any special properties, but which may prove useful in certain situations over the course of the adventure.

Most Investigators possess one starting item, representing an especially useful or cherished personal possession that can be found on their Investigator profile, which also provides you with a special rule that may prove useful at points in the adventure. These items are specific to that particular Investigator and cannot be lost, transferred, or gained.

As mentioned, other objects can be found and collected during your investigation as you journey through Innsmouth and speak with its eccentric inhabitants, but you might stumble across other objects on your journey that, unless they are notated in square brackets like your [PENCIL], alas, cannot be picked up. Record items that you can pick up on your Character Sheet but select with caution. Some items may be used to fight horrific creatures, while others might crumble the sanity you hold dear. Power corrupts, or so we're told…

CLUES AND RESOURCES

As an Investigator, you are hopefully going to uncover lots of **CLUES** along the way, as well as pick up **RESOURCES** that can help you out when things get tough. Investigators begin with **0 CLUES** and **0 RESOURCES** but can acquire them over the course of the adventure. When you acquire a **CLUE** or a **RESOURCE**, add a tally mark to the relevant box on your Character Sheet. There will be times when you have the opportunity to spend a **CLUE** or **RESOURCE** to make some of the tests or puzzles you face a little easier. If you choose to do so, strike out the appropriate number of tally marks on your Character Sheet, or reference your Investigator profile for Investigator-specific abilities regarding spending **CLUES** and **RESOURCES**.

SECRETS

Lastly, as you progress you may discover SECRETS. You will find a full list of these at the end of the gamebook. When you find a SECRET, mark it off this list. You may mark off SECRETS you discover across multiple playthroughs. If you're reading this in ebook format, you will have to keep track of the SECRETS you uncover elsewhere.

SUPER-SECRETS are also listed at the end of this gamebook. These are awarded for finishing the investigation with certain items in your position, or for having marked off various SECRETS.

READY TO BEGIN?

We certainly hope so. This is not going to be easy but finding the courage to begin is the hardest part. From here on, your chances are going to be decided by the choices you make and the path you choose to follow – not to mention skill and a little luck.

This gamebook consists of individual numbered entries. Based on your choices – or your success in various tests, challenges, and puzzles – you'll be instructed to move to a specific numbered entry at the end of each step. If you're ready to begin, turn the page, read the prologue for your chosen Investigator, and good luck. Shadow-bound Innsmouth, and the world as we know it, is in your hands.

Silas Marsh's Investigator Profile

Silas Marsh

The Sailor

Starting Item

SAILOR'S NET:
Once per adventure, while using **COMBAT**, you may immediately cancel the first dice roll and roll the dice again.

Major Ability

DRIFTER

Whenever you spend a **RESOURCE** as part of a test, if the test is successful, gain **1 RESOURCE**.

Major Weakness

SIREN'S CALL

Each time you gain **DOOM**, spend a **RESOURCE**. Otherwise, gain 1 additional **DOOM**.

Other Abilities

SAILOR
TOUGH
SURVIVOR

Other Weaknesses

TAINTED LINEAGE

Kōhaku Narukami's Investigator Profile

Kōhaku Narukami

The Folklorist

4	4	3	6	8
WILLPOWER	INTELLECT	COMBAT	HEALTH	SANITY

Starting Item

THE BOOK OF LIVING MYTHS: Once per adventure, you may substitute your **INTELLECT** for your **COMBAT** in any given fight.

Major Ability

BLESSED, CURSED

For **WILLPOWER** tests, you may roll 2 dice instead of 1, and select one of the die of your choosing. However, if the dice roll results in a double, you automatically fail and gain **1 DOOM**.

Major Weakness

WEEPING YŪREI

When you fail a **WILLPOWER** test, roll a die and add your **COMBAT**. If the total sum is equal to or less than the current **DOOM**, lose **1 HEALTH**.

Other Abilities

MYSTIC

ACADEMIC

ARCANE STUDIES

Other Weaknesses

CURSED

HAUNTED

Marion Tavares's Investigator Profile

Marion Tavares

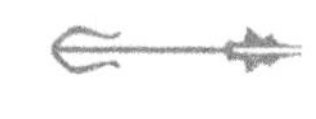

The Trawler

Starting Item

STRONG ROPE:
Once per adventure,
you may add +3 to your **WILLPOWER**.

Major Ability

DETERMINED

When using **COMBAT**, if you win a round, add an additional **+1 COMBAT** to the next round.

Major Weakness

I'LL DO IT MYSELF

Each time you lose **SANITY** or **HEALTH** roll a die. If the score is below your current **SANITY** or **HEALTH** (as appropiate), gain **+1 DOOM**. If you lose **SANITY** and **HEALTH** at the same time, choose one to apply the effect (your choice).

Other Abilities

GUARDIAN
FIGHTER
TOUGH

Other Weaknesses

CRIMINAL

SILAS

It was the first line of the advertisement that grabbed your attention as you were flicking through the newspaper: *Adventurous Individual Required.* A renowned academic needed help looking for a long-lost pirate ship. But when you saw that the ship sank off the Innsmouth coast, you decided the job wasn't for you.

You have avoided the rotting fishing town for a long time, and with good reason. There is something wrong about the place... something connected to those who share the Marsh family name.

But then the dreams returned – of alien cities hidden in the soundless depths of the ocean inhabited by inhuman horrors – and you knew then that you would never be able to rest until you faced your demons. And to do that, you must return to the town of your birth: Innsmouth.

Now turn to **22**.

KŌHAKU

It was your fascination with folklore that brought you from Boston – where your family settled after immigrating from Japan – to Arkham. But since becoming a member of the town's Historical Society, your eyes have been opened to the peculiar myths and legends of this new world.

So, when one of your fellow historians drew your attention to the advertisement in the local paper, asking for assistance in rediscovering a forgotten shipwreck in the coastal town of Innsmouth, you responded with resounding interest.

After exchanging telegrams with the academic who placed the ad, Dr Stella Addison, you soon find yourself boarding Joe Sargent's Bus Service one morning that will transport you to the mist- and myth-haunted seaside town.

Now turn to **107**.

Marion

As a seasoned trawler captain, hardened by years of hauling nets through the rough waters off the New England coast, you know you have what it takes to help Dr Stella Addison search for a lost wreck after you read the ad she placed in the *Arkham Advertiser*.

Those who know you well appreciate your sharp instincts and unyielding determination. But most do not have the slightest inkling that it is those exact qualities that earned you a missing arm while saving the life of your best friend, Grace.

You have heard many mariners' tales about Innsmouth and that particular stretch of the Atlantic coast; tales of bountiful fishing grounds and rich hauls, and darker stories concerning a cult known as the Esoteric Order of Dagon and the strange creatures that are said to dwell in the waters around Devil Reef.

Anyone looking for a sunken pirate vessel in those waters is going to need the help of someone who knows firsthand the horrors they could end up facing.

Now turn to **22**.

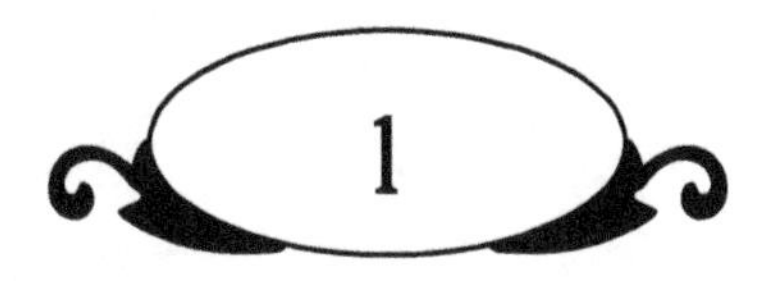

1

The fishing port of Innsmouth lies on the east coast of Massachusetts, at the mouth of the Manuxet River, like the rotting corpse of some marine leviathan washed up on shore to be picked over by crabs and carrion birds. Doomed to decline and decay until nothing of it remains apart from the skeletal vestiges of its buildings – beams bleached bone-white by the elements – it feels isolated from the rest of the world, especially by the surrounding salt marshes and its own strange, inward-looking traditions.

And yet it is to this place you have come, responding to an advertisement placed in the *Arkham Advertiser* by one Dr Stella Addison. The academic adventurer has undertaken a quest to find the wreck of a pirate ship that sank somewhere off the coast seventy years ago. This much you learned after contacting Dr Addison by telegram, which is how you also arranged to meet her at the Gilman House Hotel.

If you have the {**SAILOR**} Ability, turn to **22**.
If not, turn to **107**.

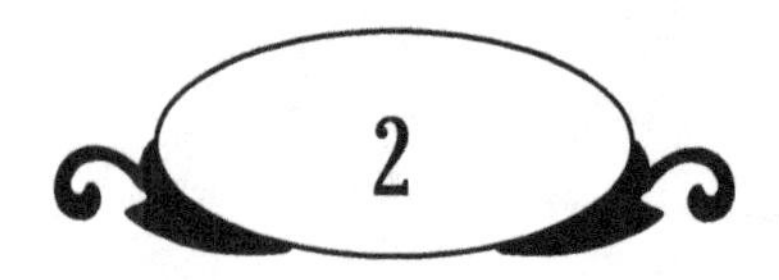

Many lose their way exploring the muddy alleyways of this decrepit backwater, but none as quickly as you.

If you are reading this because you finished the first section and simply kept on going, we must warn you that you are going to get confused very quickly, which is sure to take its toll on your sanity. This book only makes sense if you hop from entry to entry, according to the choices you make and the directions you're given. We suggest you go back and make a choice based on whether you have the **{SAILOR}** Ability or not.

Then again, maybe you're here because you think this section is the solution to one of the puzzles in the book. It isn't. Whoever said that bringing Innsmouth's secrets to the surface was going to be straightforward? However, we'll let you award yourself a Secret on this occasion. Take the SECRET: *Deep Regrets.*

Then again, perhaps you're here because you are actively trawling the book for Secrets. Not a bad tactic, and this time you've netted a prize. Take the SECRET: *Secrets of the Sea.*

> Now go back to whatever it was you were doing before, which may well mean returning to **1**.

"I know that Dr Addison had been studying the times of the tides around Innsmouth," you tell Ropes.

"And why would she be doing that then, do you think?"

Deciding you are not going to get anywhere with the policeman if you're dishonest you say, "She was searching for a pirate shipwreck, but I very much doubt that would be revealed at low tide."

"I wouldn't know about that," says the deputy constable, "but do you know what *is* revealed at low tide?"

"What?" you ask.

"The tidal tunnels, of course." The police officer smiles smugly. "They run all the way from the shore right under the town. But it's easy to get lost in that twisting labyrinth, and you don't want to find yourself stuck there at high tide." Take **+1 CLUE.**

Turn to **213**.

4

The pillars are made from the same dark stone that forms Devil Reef. And the subjects of some of the busts of jowly old men look a little... fishy.

Take the SECRET: *Hidden Six.*
Now turn back to **193** and keep reading.

5

As exotic as *Pentapods of the Abyss* sounds, it is actually a book about starfish. However, as you open the tome, it automatically settles on a page that includes information about a mythical monster called Asterias, or the Star of the Dark.

This fantastical creature was supposedly able to regenerate itself from even the smallest existing part. Being possessed of such a godlike ability meant that Asturias was worshipped by certain primitive peoples, who believed that the monstrous starfish could pass on this gift of regeneration to its disciples. Not only that, but someone in possession of a sacred amulet of Asturias could regenerate a missing body part if they, say, lost a limb or a finger. But even more incredible than that, the severed body part could grow another entire person.

Of course, such legends are pure nonsense.

Take +**1 CLUE** and the SECRET: *Hidden Five.*

Now turn back to **62** and keep reading.

6

You put up a brave defense, but the creature is too powerful. As you begin to show signs of weakening, the rest of the monsters rush forward to join in making the kill.

You soon succumb to their relentless onslaught, but you are still alive when the horrors begin to feed. Take the SECRET: *Fish Food.*

The End.

Just as you are starting to fear you are going mad, and your feelings of paranoia are all conjurations of your mind, you turn off Fish Street and walk into an ill-kept rat run called Sawbone Alley. Suddenly, two dockhands step from the shadows, knives in hand.

You do not know if they have been sent by someone to silence you or are just opportunists who intend to rob you, but you suspect it is the former. It gives you little comfort to know that you're not going mad when the evidence to the contrary involves being done over by this pair of thugs.

You may spend **1 RESOURCE** at the start of each round to add 2 to your total for that round.

Round one: roll two dice and add your **COMBAT.** If you have the Weakness **{PARANOID}**, deduct 2. If you have the **{FIGHTER}** or **{ROGUE}** Ability, add 1. If the total is 13 or more, you win the first round.

Round two: roll two dice and add your **COMBAT**. If you have the **{FIGHTER}** or **{ROGUE}** Ability, add 1. If you won the first round, add 1. If your total is 14 or more, you win the second round.

Round three: roll two dice and add your **COMBAT**. If you have the **{FIGHTER}** or **{ROGUE}** Ability, add 1. If you have the **{TOUGH}** Ability, you may also add 1. And if you won the second round, add 2. If your total is 15 or more, you win the third round.

If you won at least two rounds, turn to **190**.
If you lost at least two rounds, turn to **288**.

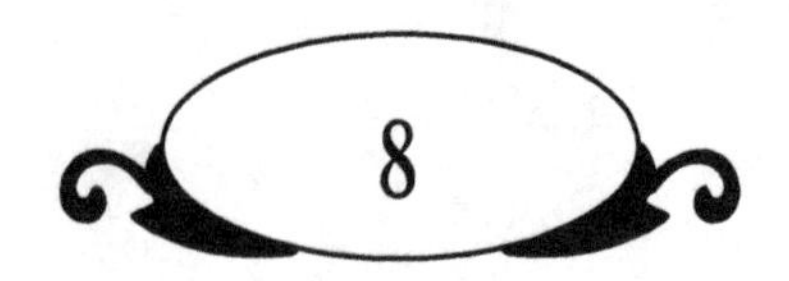

8

When you find your arms are not strong enough to haul you up the drainpipe, you try bracing yourself between the wall and the cannery. But the longer you struggle the more tired you become, until eventually you are forced to give up.

But you are not out of options yet.

If you want to try entering the cannery via the slipway, turn to **18**.

If you want to go back to the main entrance and try to bluff your way in, turn to **271**.

If you no longer want to try to gain access to the cannery, turn to **28**.

9

Your life experiences up until this point have meant you have acquired certain, ahem, *skills,* one of which proves useful to you now. Taking a split pin from your pocket and a narrow blade, you set to work picking the lock. It is not particularly complicated, and in a matter of moments you hear a click.

Turning the handle the door opens, and you enter Room #428.

Turn to **235**.

10

You do not need to be told twice and follow Dr Addison as she sprints back the way you came. She clearly knows these tunnels like the back of her hand, as she suddenly veers off along another passageway you didn't notice when you had passed it earlier.

"Don't stop!" she gasps, panting for breath. "And don't look back!"

You run on, uncaring of the sandy puddles you splash through, soaking your legs and feet.

Roll one die and deduct 1 if you have the {**AGILE**} Ability.

> If the total is equal to or less than your **HEALTH**, turn to **40**.
> If the total is greater than your **HEALTH**, turn to **30**.

11

You manage to get clear of the discarded catch of the day and waste no time in hurrying to the far end of the unloading bay, where you find an unlocked door. Take -1 **SANITY**.

Lying propped against the wall is a [**CUDGEL**] that you imagine is used to stun the fish that are brought here. If you want to take it with you, record it on your Character Sheet and gain +1 **RESOURCE**.

Getting back to the matter at hand, opening the door, you pass through it and enter the cannery proper.

Turn to **139**.

12

Dr Addison leads the way back through the tidal tunnels, brushing off any questions you have about her recent experiences and clearly not in a mood to talk about what has happened to her.

Do you have any of the following Weaknesses? {**CURSED**}, {**TAINTED LINEAGE**}, {**TROUBLED DREAMS**}?

If so, turn to **33**.
If not, turn to **54**.

Your travails in Innsmouth have taken their toll on you, both body and mind, and you never wake from the blow your enemies have dealt you. If only you had known what lay in store when you answered that fateful ad in the *Arkham Advertiser*…

The End.

According to advocates of Numerology, there is hidden power in numbers. If you add together the digits of Room #428 you get 14. Nergal, the Mesopotamian god of death, destruction, and war, was often depicted as being attended by 14 servants.

Another Mesopotamian god was Dagon, the god of fertility, who was always depicted as being half-man and half-fish.

Still, at least you're not in Room #427.

Take the SECRET: *Hidden Two*.

Now return to wherever you came here from.

15

You try to follow the same path that led you to this point, but it's no good; one outcropping of rock or patch of radiant fungus looks much like any other outcropping of rock or patch of radiant fungus.

After another half hour wandering the tunnels, you are still no closer to finding your way out. However, you press on regardless, not seeing how you can do anything other.

You eventually find yourself standing at the edge of a great, subterranean lake. Not a ripple disturbs its mirror-smooth surface, in which you can see reflected the glowing fungal growths that proliferate across the domed roof of the cavern.

But as you stare out over the lake, wondering if you will ever find your way out of this place, something whips out of the water, wraps itself around your ankle, and gives a sharp tug.

Losing your balance, you sit down hard on the ground. Something resembling a hand has a hold of your ankle, only it is a mottled green and slimy, like the skin of a frog.

In a pronounced state of shock, you watch, eyes wide with horror, as the hand releases its hold and grabs the ledge where it is swiftly joined by another. The pair then haul something from the water that is neither fish nor man, but a foul hybridization of both.

Your fight or flight response kicks in, only flight is not

possible right now. You are going to have to defend yourself from the horrid inhuman entity that has just emerged from the pool, but how?

If you want to prepare for battle, turn to **262**.
If you think you are in possession of something that might prove effective against this horror from the blue lagoon, turn to **31**.

16

The thugs lay into you with fists like hams, as well as the improvised club. Outnumbered, there is little you can do to defend yourself and ultimately succumb to their blows. They leave you in a groaning heap on the damp ground, giving you one final kick and a word of advice – "We don't take kindly to strangers in this town," – before going on their way. Take **-2 HEALTH**.

When you are sure they have gone, you slowly pick yourself up – wincing with every breath you take, as bruise after bruise reveals its presence – and hobble away down the street, unable to shake the feeling that you are still being watched by myriad watery eyes from behind the shuttered and boarded windows.

Turn to **36**.

17

Despite wracking your brains and going over all the evidence you have available to you again and again, you cannot work out where the pirate queen's treasure is hidden.

Therefore, there is only one remaining option open to you. You tell Dr Addison you are going to have to leave Innsmouth as quickly as you can, before whoever captured the academic previously comes looking for the two you.

Turn to **135**.

18

Using the wooden framework of planks and pilings that support the slipway, it is a straightforward matter to scramble up onto the ramp and follow its incline up to the shadowed opening at the top.

As you leave the chill, gray afternoon light and enter the colder gloom of the cannery's unloading bay, you believe you hear something muscular flop over in the harbor at the foot of the slipway.

You cast an anxious glance backward and while you think you can see ripples in the oily black waters, you do not catch sight of any living thing in the harbor. But you should have been looking where you were going instead.

As you step in something slimy and ever-so-slightly pliable, your initial reaction is one of revulsion. Looking down, you see that you have trodden on what appears to be waste from the day's catch that hasn't made it into tins. But your revulsion turns to shock and horror as what you thought was nothing more than a sloppy pile of dead fish and severed octopus arms moves of its own volition. Several of the rubbery appendages whip around your legs, seizing you in a crushing hold that immediately tightens.

You are not exactly sure what you are fighting against – you get the impression of fishy spines, gulping gills, and bulbous unblinking eyes, as well as cephalopod-like limbs – but fight you must.

You may spend **1 RESOURCE** at the start of each round to add 2 to your total for that round.

Round one: roll two dice and add your **COMBAT**. If you have the Weakness {**CURSED**}, deduct 2. If you have the {**FIGHTER**} or {**SAILOR**} Ability, add 1. If the total is 10 or more, you win the first round.

Round two: roll two dice and add your combat. If you have the Weakness {**CURSED**}, deduct 2. If you have the {**FIGHTER**} or {**SAILOR**} Ability, add 1. If you won the first round, add 2. If your total is 11 or more, you win the second round.

If you won the second round, turn to **11**.
If you lost the second round, turn to **98**.

19

The exact disease that wiped out half the town's populace has never been identified, but it is rumored it was brought to Innsmouth by a merchant trader.

What exactly occurred during the plague year remains a mystery to outsiders, although it is known that rioting and looting were widespread. When visitors from neighboring villages arrived, as well as finding half the townsfolk dead, they also found the Marsh family firmly in control.

Take +**1 CLUE** and the SECRET: *Hidden Seven*.

Now turn back to **107**.

20

You wander the tunnels for an hour, following whichever path feels right to you every time you encounter a branching of the ways. Usually, this means sticking to what feels like the main arterial tunnel.

You slowly become aware that the salty tang to the air has been replaced by a syrupy sweetness, until the fissured path you are following opens out into a large gallery-like space. You are somewhat taken aback to find the cave filled with all manner of large wooden barrels and chimney-like, extruded copper containers.

It takes a moment for you to realize that what you are looking at is a moonshine still, although it is not in operation at present. Taking a few minutes to discover what else is here, you find a crate of stoneware bottles that contain a previously distilled batch of liquor, as well as various tools and a coil of **[ROPE]**.

If you want to sample the moonshine, turn to **92**.
If you want to take a closer look at the tools, turn to **102**.
If you would rather pass on through the gallery, turn to **122**.

21

Extending the **[BRASS TELESCOPE]** to its fullest extent, you point it in the direction of the reef and peer through it. It takes you a moment to focus but soon you are looking at the slab of black rock directly.

There are all sorts of old mariner tales about Devil Reef. Some say that the richest fishing waters in the whole of New England surround the outcrop, while others claim that it sometimes vanishes from view before reappearing suddenly and threatening nearby vessels as a result. However, what is undeniable fact is that the "reef" isn't formed from coral but a black, possibly volcanic, rock, making it anomalous compared to the rest of the Innsmouth coast.

And then you see something... but only for a moment before it is gone again. You continue to peer through the lens, trying to locate it again, but it is no longer there. Perhaps it was never there and what you thought you saw was no more than an optical illusion, a trick of the light. Only you were sure you saw the silhouette of something like a man dive from the reef into the waves as the telescope swept across the mysterious landmark. Take **-1 SANITY.**

"Come on!" Dr Addison snaps. "We're wasting time." She always seems to be in such a hurry. "We need to getout to the reef now!"

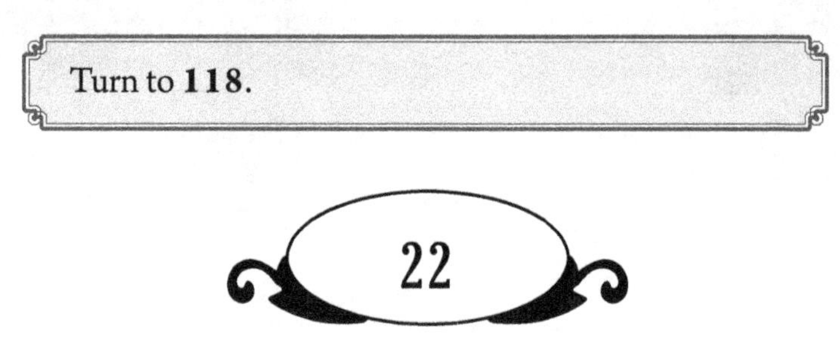

Turn to **118**.

22

Innsmouth is almost cut off from its neighboring towns by the treacherous marshes and brackish creeks surrounding it, and the only way in and out of the town by land is via the coastal highway, which is as neglected and decrepit as the rest of the town's infrastructure. It is far more convenient to access the town from the sea, especially when you have your own boat.

While the sky overhead is overcast, the fog that seems to almost perpetually blanket the town is thankfully absent. That, and a relatively calm sea, makes navigation a far easier task than it might be. Avoiding the treacherous shoals of Devil Reef, you bring your boat into Innsmouth Harbor without any trouble.

The jetties, wharves, and derricks are a rotting reminder of how grand the harbor used to be. The shells of abandoned warehouses cling to the harborside like limpets and the flaking planks and posts of the piers that remain are smothered with lank seaweed and clusters of bivalves.

You moor your vessel among those already at rest along the southern edge of the harbor, as close to the breakwater as possible. Grabbing a pack containing some supplies, you disembark. Take +3 **RESOURCES**.

At any other fishing port along the coast of New England you would expect to see the harbor area teeming with stevedores and mariners at this time, but Innsmouth Harbor appears almost deserted. Those fishermen you do see huddled together on the quayside, smoking their pipes and muttering to one another in their almost incomprehensible local dialect, stare at you blankly with the same unblinking, slack-faced expressions.

But there is one old sea dog who doesn't share this curious "Innsmouth look." His lean and tattered form gives him the appearance of a scarecrow instead. While he may appear normal to you, he also seems to be talking to himself. But when he catches sight of you, he waves you over.

If you want to stop and talk to the old man, turn to **42**.
If you would prefer to head into town for your rendezvous with Dr Addison, turn to **63**.

23

"I was supposed to meet Dr Addison at the Gilman House Hotel," you explain to the duty constable, "but she never showed. I managed to gain entry to her room" – at this remark, Deputy Constable Ropes raises a suspicious eyebrow – "and found her diary. But the only thing written in there that might be relevant were the names of two locations: 'Tidal Tunnels' and 'The Little Bookshop.'"

"And have you tried looking for this Dr Addison at either of those places?" Deputy Constable Ropes puts down his pen and looks at you pointedly. You get the impression he couldn't care less about what has become of the errant academic. Take **+1 CLUE.**

Turn to **213**.

24

The quickest way to reach Falcon Point from Innsmouth is by sea. It's not a long walk to the harbor, where you moored your boat upon arriving at the fishing town.

If you want to suggest to Dr Addison that you would do best to travel by sea, turn to **117**.
If you think it is too risky, considering the encroaching fog and the imminent approach of night, turn to **224**.

25

"I was supposed to meet her at the Gilman House Hotel," you explain once you have revealed your reason for visiting Innsmouth today. "You wouldn't happen to have seen her, would you?"

"Medium height, with tight red curls?" Joyce asks you, her eyes narrowing in suspicion.

You have never met Stella Addison, having only communicated via telegram thus far, but you nod anyway.

"No!" Joyce Little suddenly snaps.

Confused, you say, "She might have popped in here looking for information about shipwrecks off the Massachusetts coast, or books on local history."

"No, I am sure I would have remembered if she had."

"But you described–"

"Is that the time?" the woman says, pushing past you without even looking at the clock on the wall and opening the door. "I'm closing now. Goodbye."

You consider resisting the woman's urging, but in the end decide you have learned something of use anyway. Take **+1 CLUE.**

Turn to **35**.

Without any further delay, the two of you leave the hotel. Descending the steps from the lobby, you head to the Town Square, your eyes seeking out the bus stop, but there is no bus there.

You must get out of town and fast. Bearing in mind that where you ran into trouble was north of the Manuxet River, your surest ways out of Innsmouth have to be to the south along the coast road to Arkham, or by sea via the harbor.

Looking east in the direction of the harbor, you are horrified to see a thick sea fog rolling in from the ocean. Dusk is already falling, but the advancing blackish-green smog is smothering everything within the fishing town, and even dimming the streetlamps that are just coming on.

"Come on!" snaps Dr Addison. "We cannot delay any longer. We can't let a little fog delay us." And so, you begin to make your way out of town.

However, as the fog first blurs and then absorbs the surrounding buildings, thereby robbing you of any useful landmarks and stealing away your natural sense of direction, you become aware of other things moving within the murk. You spot one and then soon after a second and a third, and before long you come to the chilling realization that you are surrounded by shadowy figures.

The lumpen forms appear to be human, or at least humanoid, walking upright on two legs, although you strain to make out any more details. However, it is the strange cries echoing through the fog that raise your heart rate and the hackles on the back of your neck.

You can hear an amphibian croaking, an indefinable

hooting, and unintelligible gibbering. Then there are the voices; they sound like they are coming from throats clogged with phlegm and not in any language you can understand.

You keep close to Dr Addison but out here on the streets of the decaying fishing town, in the clammy grip of the all-enveloping miasma, you feel a creeping sense of dread and a cold knot of fear forms in the pit of your stomach. Then all your worst fears come to fruition as the figures close in around you. You see their hairless, slack-jawed faces and watery wide-set eyes, and you know then that you will never escape this cursed town. Slimy hands seize you and a split second later something hits you across the back of the head and you lose consciousness. Take -**1 HEALTH**.

Roll one die and deduct 1 if you have the **{SURVIVOR}** or **{TOUGH}** Ability.

If the total is equal to or less than your **HEALTH**, turn to **298**.
If the total is greater than your **HEALTH**, turn to **13**.

27

The old man doesn't appear to have moved since you were last here, but now he's ranting drunkenly, with himself as the only audience. That is, until he sets his blurry eyes upon you. A look of intense concentration wrinkles his features and then, with something like recognition, he directs his angry tirade at you.

"Dun't believe me, hey? Then jest tell me, young feller, why Cap'n Obed an' twenty odd other folks used to row aout to Devil Reef in the dead o' night an' chant things so laoud ye cud hear 'em all over taown when the wind was right?"

Captain Obed? Devil Reef? Strange midnight chanting? What is the old drunkard going on about?

If you want to engage him in conversation again, turn to **283**.
If you think you'll hear nothing good if you do, turn to **294**.

28

The sky above the town is covered by a featureless gray pall and looking out to sea, you can see even darker clouds massing on the horizon.

Choosing somewhere you haven't been already, where do you want to go now in your quest for information?

Henderson's Oddities: turn to **45**.
The Little Bookshop: turn to **91**.
Down to the shore: turn to **126**.
The Innsmouth Harbor: turn to **82**.
The Innsmouth Cannery: turn to **281**.
If there is an alternative location you would like to visit, turn to **170**.

29

You take the lump of gold from your pack and hold it up so the fish-men can see it. They freeze instantly, their eyes on the object in your hand.

"You want this, do you?" you bellow over the roar of the sea and the keening howl of the wind.

You go to cast the lustrous pebble into the sea and the fish-men all jerk, ready to spring in the same direction, as if they would be ready to dive in after it.

"Go on, then!" you say and hurl the lump of metal as far as you can off the port side of the boat.

As anticipated, all three of the hunting fish-things leap into the sea after it and vanish from sight as they are swallowed by the dark waves.

Strike the [**SEA GOLD**] from your Character Sheet and take -**1 DOOM**.

Your quick thinking has got you out of a tight spot! Take +**1 INTELLECT**.

Turn to **174**.

30

Your travails in Innsmouth have taken their toll and you just don't have the stamina to escape the pursuing horrors.

You can hear the slapping of their feet on the rocky floor, while their gurgling voices echo through the network of tunnels. And then, when the fishy reek of them reaches your nostrils, with Dr Addison disappearing ahead of you, you feel rough, clawed hands seize you.

Something hits you on the back of the head and you crash to the ground. Take -**1 HEALTH** and -**1 COMBAT**.

As consciousness fades, several of your pursuers hop past you and moments later you hear a cry and know that the fish-men have caught up with the academic as well.

Roll one die and deduct 1 if you have the {**SURVIVOR**} or {**TOUGH**} Ability.

If the total is equal to or less than your **HEALTH**, turn to **298**.
If the total is greater than your **HEALTH**, turn to **13**.

31

What do you have that you think could prove to be an effective weapon against the horror?

If you are in possession of one of the following, you could try using it now.

> [CARVED IDOL]: turn to **52**.
> [SEA GOLD]: turn to **72**.
> If you do not have either of these items, or do not want to use them now, turn to **262**.

32

Ultimately, you succeed in sending each of the repulsive, slimy fish-men back into the ocean, while Dr Addison does exactly what you told her to do. You made the right call in giving her the wheel so you could battle the horrors! Take **+1 INTELLECT**.

> Turn to **174**.

As the two of you make your way through the natural labyrinth, you can't shake the feeling that you are being followed. As the intensity of the feeling grows, you open your mouth to tell Dr Addison your suspicions when she suddenly comes to an abrupt halt. She doesn't say anything, but just points.

There, ahead of you, limned by the unreal light of the glowing fungi that cover the ceiling, you can see a gaggle of shadowy figures scampering toward you. They are bipedal, but their loping gait gives you the impression that they are not used to walking. Indeed, one of them is moving along the passage more like a frog.

The danger wasn't behind you, it was ahead of you all the time.

If you stay where you are, you are going to have to confront the creatures. But if you run back the way you have come, who knows how long it will be before you ever find your way out of these godforsaken tunnels.

"Run!" Dr Addison hisses, pulling on your arm.

If you want to do as Dr Addison says and flee, turn to **10**.
If you would rather stand and face whatever is hunting you, turn to **247**.

34

You think you have a pretty good idea where Dr Addison might have gone and decide that it is time to put your theory to the test.

If you think you know where Dr Addison has gone, turn the two-word location name into numbers using the code A=1, B=2 ... Z=26, and add them up.

A	B	C	D	E	F	G	H	I	J
1	2	3	4	5	6	7	8	9	10
K	**L**	**M**	**N**	**O**	**P**	**Q**	**R**	**S**	**T**
11	12	13	14	15	16	17	18	19	20
U	**V**	**W**	**X**	**Y**	**Z**				
21	22	23	24	25	26				

However, you should also have a time connected to the location. Taking the hours as one number and the minutes as another number, add these two numbers up. Then, add that sum to the sum you've calculated after converting the location name into numbers. Then, turn to the same section as the final total.

If the section you turn to makes no sense, turn to **65**.

35

Leaving The Little Bookshop, you consider where to go next in your search for information concerning Dr Stella Addison's current whereabouts. Spend either 1 clue or 1 resource or take **+1 DOOM.**

Considering what you have already learned and choosing somewhere you haven't visited already, where do you want to go now?

Henderson's Oddities: turn to **45**.
Down to the shore: turn to **126**.
The Innsmouth Harbor: turn to **82**.
The Innsmouth Cannery: turn to **281**.
If there is an alternative location you would like to visit, turn to **170**.

36

It is with no small measure of relief that you finally find a way out of the warren of rat runs onto Main Street, and from there you make your way to the cobbled Town Square.

A branch of the First National Grocery chain stands on the square, while a signpost points the way to the Gilman House Hotel.

> If you want to enter the First National Grocery, turn to **160**.
> If you want to head to the Gilman House Hotel to meet with Dr Addison, turn to **83**.

37

Simply looking at some of the strange artifacts makes you feel queasy, but at the same time you feel a strange desire to pick one up.

Which of the curiosities do you want to examine more closely?

> One of the hand-carved idols: turn to **47**.
> The white-gold statuary: turn to **57**.
> One of the even more unusual objets d'art: turn to **67**.

38

Making it to the top of the wall you look down into the enclosed space below. While it is full of the sort of detritus you might expect to find somewhere like this – splintered wooden crates, heaps of old rope, rusted chains – you cannot see any of the employees of the plant anywhere nearby, and so you use a conveniently stacked pile of pallets to aid your descent.

When you reach the ground, lying across the top of an opened crate is a [**CROWBAR**]. If you want to take it with you, record it on your Character Sheet and gain **+1 RESOURCE.**

A shadowy doorway leads from the yard into the cannery itself, so that is the way you go now.

Turn to **139**.

39

Pulling the grotesque figure from your pack, you thrust it toward the fish-men.

If you were hoping they would be cowed by the graven image or prostrate themselves before it, you are sadly mistaken.

The nearest bares its needle-sharp teeth and an angry hiss escapes its malformed mouth. Before you know what is going on, the monster throws itself at you and is quickly joined by its companions, so you find yourself having to deal with all three of them.

You may spend **1 RESOURCE** at the start of each round, but only from the second round of combat onwards, to add 2 to your total for that round.

Round one: roll two dice and add your **COMBAT**, but then deduct the current **DOOM** level. If you have the {**TOUGH**} Ability, add 1. If the total is 15 or more, you win the first round.

Round two: roll two dice and add your **COMBAT**. If you have the {**AGILE**} Ability, add 1. If you won the first round, add 2. If your total is 16 or more, you win the second round.

Round three: roll two dice and add your **COMBAT**. If you have the {**FIGHTER**} Ability, add 1. If you won the first round, add 2. If your total is 17 or more, you win the second round.

If you won at least two rounds, turn to **90**.
If you lost two or more rounds, turn to **53**.

You manage to keep pace with the nimble Dr Addison, the rush of adrenaline providing power to your legs, and you eventually find yourselves traversing a long tunnel that doesn't veer to the left or right but keeps going straight. Both of you feel fatigued and your run slows to a jog until your jog becomes a walk, which eventually brings you to a flight of stone steps.

Climbing the steps you emerge inside the ruined shell of what turns out to be the lighthouse that stands at the end of the harbor breakwater. Navigating the debris of broken timbers you finally manage to extract yourselves from the ruin.

Free from the tidal tunnels and your pursuers, for the time being at least, the two of you make your way through the streets as the evening light starts to wane.

Turn to **75**.

41

You try the handle again, but the door remains firmly locked.

If you have the {**ROGUE**} Ability or the {**CRIMINAL**} Weakness, turn to **9**.
If not, turn to **295**.

42

You make your way over to where the old man is sitting on a lobster pot and wish him a good day.

His face suddenly darkens and he stabs an accusing finger in your face. "What ye think ye doin', moorin' yer boat on this godforsaken shore?"

Smelling the liquor on his breath, you understand what has given his anger such a strong voice. But it is more than just anger; it is fear as well.

"Git out! This town is cursed! Git back on yer boat and be gone, else you'll find yourself down at the bottom of the briny deep feeding the fish or cavortin' with the rest of them."

The old man's fury unsettles you. Perhaps it is the curious appearance of the other Innsmouth fishermen, but on hearing the sea dog's words your mind suddenly fills with visions of twisted creatures gathered in a great tumult at the bottom of the sea, where they squirm and writhe like a knot of hagfish. But they aren't fish. They are something much worse, for they are both humanoid in appearance and yet, at the same time, far less than human. Take **-1 SANITY** but **+1 CLUE**.

"Get away from me, old timer," you say, backing away.

"Well, if you won't leave," he says, pulling a bottle wrapped in a brown paper bag from a deep coat pocket and thrusting it toward you, "take this. And don't say I didn't warn you."

The reek of alcohol is strong. If you want to take the bottle of **[WHISKEY]**, record it on your Character Sheet and take **+1 RESOURCE**.

Take the SECRET: *Drunk and Disorderly.*

Turn to **63**.

"I was supposed to meet Dr Addison at the Gilman House Hotel," you explain to the duty constable, "but she never showed. I managed to gain entry to her room" – at this Deputy Constable Ropes raises a suspicious eyebrow – "and I found a copy of the *Innsmouth Tribune* among her things. It was folded open on an article about seismic activity that has been recorded in the area and another concerning the new cannery."

"Ah yes," says Ropes, "another venture undertaken by the beneficent Marsh family. Old Man Marsh and his kin have done a lot for this town; more than you'll ever know. If your friend really has gone missing, you can be sure it has nothing to do with the Innsmouth Cannery or the Marsh family."

You don't like the police officer's tone. Take the Weakness **{WATCHED}**.

Turn to **213**.

As soon as the cultists see the **[SEA GOLD]**, they slow their steps, and a low murmuring fills the chamber.

What do you want to do now that you appear to have the advantage?

Make your last stand against the Order: turn to **116**.
Get out of there while you still can: turn to **274**.

Like much of the rest of the town, Martin Street is a patchwork of crumbling facades, filth-obscured windows, and boarded-up doorways. But this only makes Henderson's Oddities that much easier to locate; first the sign hanging outside the shop, bearing a golden anchor, and then the lights shining from its sparkling windows, acting on you like a sea devil's lure, until you are standing inside the shop marveling at the wonders within.

The shop is filled with all kinds of paraphernalia – some of it familiar, some of it less so – that is either crammed into racks of shelves, hanging from the ceiling beams, or just piled on the floor.

Standing behind the counter is a strapping young man with a mane of luxurious blond hair. He looks curiously out of place in this palace of curiosities, and you can't help feeling he would be more at home on a football field.

Nevertheless, as you enter Henderson's Oddities, he welcomes you with a smile. "Is there anything I can do for you?" he asks.

If you have the {**SAILOR**} Ability, turn to **74**.
If not, turn to **94**.

46

You suddenly hear a noise outside the door.

"They're here!" Dr Addison hisses, a look of wide-eyed shock on her face. "What shall we do?"

You desperately look around you, searching for a solution, such as an alternative way out.

There is the window that looks out over a cobbled courtyard, which frustratingly lies three stories below, but there are also two connecting doors, joining Room #428 to the bedroom to the north and the one to the south, which you didn't notice the last time you were here.

As you are trying to decide what to do, someone tries the door from the hallway. You are going to have to act fast.

What do you want to do?

Open the door and fight your way past whoever is outside: turn to **110**.
Use the window as a means of escape: turn to **157**.
Barge open one of the adjoining doors and make your escape that way: turn to **217**.

47

The curious effigies are carved from some exotic hardwood, the sort of timber that was so popular in the last century and that travelers would bring back from such far-flung places as Java and Fiji. But there are no further resemblances beyond that.

The effigies all appear to be an unholy amalgam of human and fish, and each one you consider is more hideous than the last. But the most repugnant of them all has the piscine qualities of its fellows replaced with those of a cephalopod. It is posed to look like it is squatting on a plinth and has a great pair of dragon-like wings folded across its back. Despite its monstrous appearance, you cannot resist the draw of its dark majesty.

However, you cannot just take it. If you wish to take the [CARVED IDOL] with you, you will have to exchange it for **1 RESOURCE**.

Whether you acquire the [CARVED IDOL] or not, what do you want to do next?

Study the white-gold statuary: turn to **57**.
Pick up one of the more unusual objets d'art: turn to **67**.
Leave Henderson's Oddities: turn to **84**.

48

As you flee, you stumble – when a puddle turns out to be a pothole – and collide with a broken barrel full of filthy rainwater. The steel hoops holding the barrel together are corroded and covered in flakes of rust. You graze your side against the barrel, your fear of who – or what – might be following you stifling your cry of pain. Take -1 **HEALTH**.

Picking yourself up, the cries of seabirds circling overhead accompany your flight through the stinking streets of the Shoreward Slums.

Turn to **36**.

49

The two police officers give you a beating worthy of mob enforcers before throwing you into a solitary cell. Take -2 **HEALTH**.

It's time to make a **HEALTH** check. Roll one die and deduct 1 if you have the **{SURVIVOR}** or **{TOUGH}** Ability.

If the total is equal to or less than your **HEALTH**, turn to **79**.
If the total is greater than your **HEALTH**, turn to **59**.

50

Stretching back your arm, you cast the [GREENSTONE STATUE] out to sea as Dr Addison screams in distraught horror. It sails through the air, describing an arcing parabola over the heads of the fish-horde and lands with a silent splash amid the whitewater boiling around the surfacing leviathan.

There is a moment where nothing happens other than the incessant rain of the cascading water, and then the assembled fish-things hiss in unison, a triumphant sound, and race up the beach toward you and the beleaguered Dr Addison.

Faced with such overwhelming odds, you refuse to let them end you on the beach without taking at least some of them with you.

Defiant to the last, you are still able to witness when the horrors make an offering of you to Father Dagon.

Take the SECRET: *Father Dagon.*

Final score: 0 stars.

The End.

51

Pulling one of your possessions from your pack, you thrust it toward the fish-men. The nearest one lashes out, striking the object from your hand and sending it sailing into the sea.

Strike one [**ITEM**] from your Character Sheet. If you do not have any [**ITEMS**], take -**1 RESOURCE**. It is lost to you forever.

The monsters launch themselves at you, and you suddenly find yourself having to deal with all three together.

You may spend **1 RESOURCE** at the start of each round, but only from the second round of combat onward, to add 2 to your total for that round.

Round one: roll two dice and add your **COMBAT**, but then deduct the current doom level. If you have the {**TOUGH**} Ability, add 1. If the total is 15 or more, you win the first round.

Round two: roll two dice and add your **COMBAT**. If you have the {**AGILE**} Ability, add 1. If you won the first round, add 2. If your total is 16 or more, you win the second round.

Round three: roll two dice and add your **COMBAT**. If you have the {**FIGHTER**} Ability, add 1. If you won the first round, add 2. If your total is 17 or more, you win the second round.

If you won at least two rounds, turn to **90**.
If you lost two or more rounds, turn to **53**.

Taking out the hideous carving, which is as grotesque as the monster you are facing, you brandish it before the fish-man.

The creature hisses at you in fury and recoils. But in the next moment, it lashes out with one clawed appendage, swiping the carving from your hand. It lands in the pool with a splash, while blood runs from a slash across your forearm.

Take -1 **HEALTH** and strike the **[CARVED IDOL]** from your Character Sheet.

Still hissing, the creature advances toward you with murderous intent and then launches a savage attack.

Turn to **262**.

You fight valiantly against the invaders, but unfortunately it is not enough.

One of the foul-smelling creatures wraps its long limbs around you, pinning your arms to your sides, and throws itself back over the side of the ship.

As you hit the water, the bone-numbing cold steals the breath from your lungs in an instant. With frog-like kicks of its powerful legs, the creature takes you down into the ocean's pitch-black depths, deeper and deeper, until the pressure in your lungs becomes unbearable and you open your mouth to take a breath…

Freezing seawater pours into your throat and precious, life-giving air escapes your lungs as dark oblivion swallows your world.

The End.

54

Finally, you enter a cave that leads to the sea. The rising tide has half-filled the chamber already. Dr Addison doesn't hesitate in running into the surf and splashing through the calf-deep water, and out through the cave mouth. You follow close on her sodden heels.

You have made it out of the tidal tunnels and rescued Dr Addison from whatever fate awaited her. Take the SECRET: *Dr Addison, I Presume.*

The striking redhead gives the overcast sky a wary look before saying, "We're running out of time. We have to get back to the hotel before dark."

And so the two of you leave the sinister shoreline and head through the streets of Innsmouth for the Gilman House Hotel once more, as the sun continues its inexorable journey toward the western horizon behind banks of gray clouds.

Turn to **75**.

55

Something deep within your soul answers the gold's siren call. You cannot resist and fill your pockets with as much of the [**SEA GOLD**] as you can carry.

Record the [**SEA GOLD**] on your Character Sheet and take +**2 DOOM**. You may spend **1 CLUE** or **1 RESOURCE** to reduce the doom penalty by 1; spend **2 CLUES** or **2 RESOURCES** to avoid adding any doom.

Turn to **178**.

56

Taking your seat on the mildewed couch once more, under the watchful gaze of the hotelier, you continue to wait in the hope that he will have to leave his post eventually, if only for a brief comfort break.

Time drags while you wait, the hands of the clock in the lobby moving at an apparent snail's pace. But thankfully, the moment does eventually come, although you are forced to endure thirty minutes of ennui before it does, which saps your will. Take -**1 WILLPOWER**.

As the man slips away to some back room, you do not waste a second. Lifting the counter hatch and sneaking behind the desk, you find the key you are looking for, take it from the rack, and hurry back upstairs. Upon reaching the top floor again, you insert the key into the lock and hear a satisfying click as you give it a turn.

Turn to **235**.

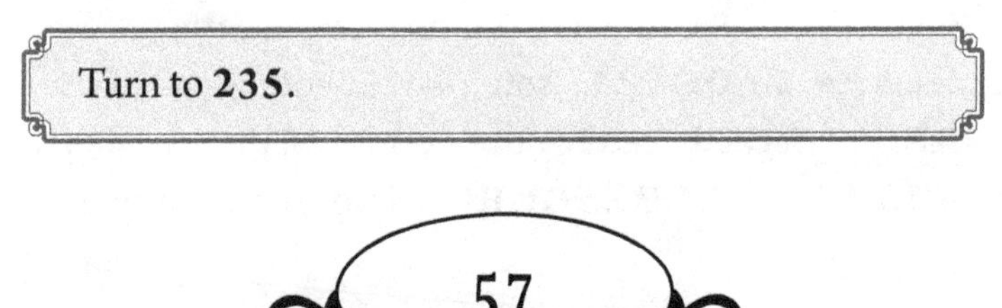

57

You suppose the metal the statues are made from is valuable, but it's not like anything you've seen before. It has a curious luster, like gold but which also puts you in mind of mother-of-pearl. In fact, you could almost believe that the statuary has been washed white by the sea after being submerged in the cold, black depths of the eternal ocean.

The figurines do not have any clearly defined shape – they

might be fish or people, or nothing more than extruded ingots – but there are other things made of the seemingly precious metal too, things that put you in mind of arm rings, necklaces and crowns.

Jack Henderson will not simply give away his sea gold collection and many of the items are worth far more than you can afford, but no doubt he will let you have one of the shapeless lumps for 2 resources.

If you do "buy" one of the pieces, turn to **161**.
If not, you could take a closer look at the carved idols, if you haven't already: turn to **47**.
Or you could take a look at one of the more unusual items on offer: turn to **67**.
But if you want to leave Henderson's Oddities, turn to **84**.

58

You hold the [OCTOPUS CROWN] above your head and, as one, the cultists prostrate themselves on the ground before you.

You're not going to get a better chance than this one to get out of here, and so you take it. Take +1 **SANITY**.

Turn to **200**.

59

Locked in a cell and with no hope of escape, your fate will ultimately be decided by Chief Constable Andrew Martin and Deputy Constable Carey Ropes, or, more likely, their Marsh family masters. But whatever befalls you, your adventure is over.

Take the SECRET: *Banged Up*.

The End.

60

As you cast your eyes over the strange runes, you feel a small portion of the power contained within the statue transfer into you. Take +1 **COMBAT**, +1 **INTELLECT**, and +1 **WILLPOWER**.

Take the SECRET: *Hidden Four*.

Now turn back to **289** and read on.

61

"What happens on April 30 and October 31?" you ask Brian.

He shushes you, keeping a wary eye on his other clientele.

"They say those are the two nights of the year when evil can walk abroad freely and those who are wise stay indoors. They have been celebrated by pagan peoples for millennia."

"And the people of Innsmouth?"

"Oh, far longer than that."

You are certainly less keen to remain in Innsmouth overnight after speaking with the young entrepreneur. Take +1 **CLUE** and -1 **SANITY**, and the SECRET: *Hidden One*.

Turn to **259**.

62

All manner of esoteric titles seems to spring out at you from the shelves. They have lurid titles such as *Dark Rites of the Dark Woods*, *Pentapods of the Abyss*, and *The Mists of Kingsport*, but one of the titles among this list stands out more than any other. Then, another title commands your complete attention. Perhaps it is because you subconsciously feel you have come across a certain name somewhere before: *A True History of the Esoteric Order of Dagon*.

Scanning its pages, you lose several minutes reviewing its wild claims. According to the book's author, one Phillip Howard, the Esoteric Order of Dagon was reportedly founded in the mid-1800s after Captain Obed Marsh returned from a long sea voyage. It was focused on the veneration of Dagon, an ancient sea deity, to secure prosperity from the sea. But what started out as something akin to a Masonic lodge gradually evolved into something even more secretive and mysterious, which indulged in sinister practices and celebrated such pagan festivals as Beltane and Samhain. The author claims to know the details of some of those rites and has recorded them within this book.

Take +**2 CLUES** and the SECRET: *Something Fishy*.

Record the **{SECRET RITES}** Ability on your Character Sheet.

Turn to **239**.

63

The fishing town is a mere shadow of what it used to be a century ago. Decades of neglect have left the once impressive public and private buildings of that time in a state of disrepair and near total collapse for many. It has nothing to offer the outside world. There is no university as there is in Arkham, no hospital such as the one in Kingsport, and the railway companies stopped coming to Innsmouth long ago.

That said, three tall steeples loom above the sagging roofs and fallen facades of the surrounding buildings, although even the top of one of these has collapsed, and in another there are gaping black holes where clock dials must once have been.

If you have the Weakness **{TAINTED LINEAGE}**, turn to **83**.
If not, turn to **114**.

The young man readily agrees and, as he switches the radio on, you make your introductions – he is Japheth Henderson, the owner of the curiosity shop, although those who know him better call him "Jack."

As the radio crackles to life, the tinfoil crunch of static fades to a background hum as Jack manipulates the tuning dial.

"This is Jack Henderson of Innsmouth," he says into the microphone as he depresses the button to speak. "Is there anyone out there?"

When he releases the button again, you fancy you can hear a gaggle of voices beneath the eerie whoops and wails of the distorted signal. Straining to filter out the white noise in an effort to pick out one distinct voice, you are startled when a desperate plea suddenly cuts through all other chatter.

"Mayday! Mayday! This is the… zzzkkkzzz…"

The voice is drowned by a wave of static only to resurface a moment later. "… ack! I repeat, we are under atta… zzkkkzzz… anybody hear me?"

Jack scrambles to hit the speak button. "Yes, I can hear you! What's your position?"

For a moment there is nothing but the swirl of static until the voice returns once more.

"… zzkk… degrees west. Devil Reef is… zzzkkk… to port."

The signal breaks up one last time, and Jack fiddles with the dial again to improve the signal. He only manages to recover the signal for one brief moment before it is lost to the sea of static. All you hear in that split second is a bloodcurdling scream.

When it becomes clear that he has lost all contact with the unknown vessel, Jack switches off the radio.

The two of you look at each other sickly, your shocked expressions saying everything that needs to be said.

Deeply unsettled, with a muttered farewell you leave the curiosity shop in haste. Outside, you come to a shaking halt, your heart racing, your mind whirling, and a nauseous feeling rising from the pit of your stomach.

Take -**1** **SANITY** and +**1** **DOOM**, along with the SECRET: *Dead Signal.*

Turn to **84**.

Clearly you need to keep searching for clues as to Dr Addison's current whereabouts.

Choosing somewhere you haven't visited already, where do you want to go now?

Henderson's Oddities: turn to **45**.
The Little Bookshop: turn to **91**.
Down to the shore: turn to **126**.
The Innsmouth Harbor: turn to **82**.
The Innsmouth Cannery: turn to **281**.
Alternatively, perhaps it's time you asked for aid in finding the missing academic. Turn to **108**.
But if you are completely out of ideas as to where to look, turn to **299**.

66

Your attacker has the high ground and therefore, the advantage. But as he makes another lunge with the boat hook, you seize its rusty tip and pull. Unbalanced, the man stumbles toward you and as he does so, you grab hold of the lapels of his coat and swing him out over the edge of the cliff.

What follows is a moment of scrabbling panic as you begin to lose your balance as well, and your feet have an unsteady grip on the slick rock. You clutch at anything in an attempt to arrest your fall, and fortunately it works. Take the Weakness **{FEAR OF HEIGHTS}**.

But it is too late for your wild attacker. The man drops like a stone toward the savage rocks, only to be caught by a wave as it crashes against the cliff, and swallowed by the great swirl of foam-flecked black water.

When the wave recedes again, there is no sign of the man's body, either broken on the stony beach or floating face down in the sea.

Take the SECRET: *Lost at Sea.*

Dr Addison shows only the barest interest in your well-being before urging you to press on down the perilous path.

Turn to **255**.

There are fossils of ammonites, ancient shark teeth, and arachnids trapped in resin. And that's just a few of the curios on display. But then something else catches your eye.

At first glance, you take it to be an old leather glove, but when you remove it from the shelf you realize it is a mummified hand. That revelation is surprise enough but when, morbidly fascinated, you study it closely under one of the shop lamps, you begin to suspect that the owner of the hand didn't, in fact, suffer from psoriasis, and that what you first took to be flaking skin is actually scales. Not only that, but the fingers are joined by great webs of skin.

In a flash, you are no longer standing, dumbstruck, in Henderson's Oddities but at the bottom of the ocean. But you aren't drowning, you're swimming between great stacks of rock with ease and apparently without the need to breathe. And then, just as abruptly, you are back in the curiosity shop.

Take -**1 SANITY** and the SECRET: *Full Fathom Five.*

You are so shaken by your experience with the hand that you cannot bear to remain here a moment longer. And so, without a word to the shopkeeper, you quit Henderson's Oddities as fast as you can, your pulse racing.

Turn to **84**.

68

"That way," the thug says, using the plank of wood he is carrying to indicate the route you should take. "Now be gone with you."

You don't wait to be told twice and set off in the direction the bruiser indicated. You can feel their watery eyes on you all the way to the end of the street.

Turn to **36**.

69

The solid stone slab that passes for a bed is so uncomfortable that after half an hour you get up and start pacing around the cell. Your attention turns to your feet, and it is then that you notice a distinct crack in the floor. Tiles have been set into the floor and secured with mortar. But the mortar is missing where the "bed" makes contact with the ground.

Your curiosity piqued, you give the stone slab an experimental tug. With the echoing grating of stone, it shifts. You freeze, your heart racing, convinced that the police officers will come running at any moment. But when they do not make an appearance, emboldened, you heave on the slab a second time. This time it moves halfway across the cell, revealing a yawning hole beneath it.

Not waiting to find out if the policemen heard the noise

created by your endeavors this time, your heart thudding against your ribs, you screw your courage to the sticking place and slide through the hole feetfirst.

You drop only a matter of six feet or so and land in a crouch. The muted daylight filtering through the windows of the jail above informs you that you are in a circular tunnel hewn from earth and rock. Ahead, a pale glow seems to beckon you forward. Behind waits the stone-cold cell and an uncertain fate.

There really is no choice to be made at all and so you set off in the direction of the will-o'-the-wisp-like luminescence.

As you reach the limit of the pale, gray daylight's reach, you are surprised to find the way ahead suffused with a bioluminescent blue glow. Intrigued, you continue along the tunnel as it becomes a natural fissure in the rock. You soon discover the source of the bioluminescence; it is produced by not one, but a plethora of different types of fungi that you have never come across anywhere else. They must be indigenous to this stretch of the New England coast.

Farther on again, the passageway you are following joins a larger tunnel, and you find yourself walking on sand. You can see the grooves of drag marks in the sand, but they do not give you any indication which way you should go now.

So, what's it to be?

To go right, turn to **152**.
To go left, turn to **186**.

The pirate ship sank seventy years ago. But why? And what was it carrying that Dr Addison is so eager to get her hands on? Are the answers to these questions connected in some way? Your imagination runs wild with possibilities. But if you and the academic were to find the wreck of the Chinese junk yourselves… why, that would be a discovery for the ages!

Take +**1 CLUE** and the SECRET: *Hidden Three*.

Now return to wherever you came here from.

Running a hand along the bookshelves, you find yourself picking out the name of the town with increasing frequency. You stop and pull a few of the volumes from a shelf. But the one that really piques your interest is called *Innsmouth: The Rise and Fall of a Fishing Town.*

Reading the preface, you discover that it details Innsmouth in the last century, and how its fortunes were transformed almost overnight by the mysterious plague that struck in the 1840s. Take the SECRET: *Ghost Town*.

Flicking through it further, you find that someone – a previous owner of the book, perhaps – has used a folded piece of paper as a bookmark at the start of a chapter about bootleggers. But when you unfold it out of curiosity, you discover that it is a hand-drawn map of what would appear to be a network of tunnels.

Take **+1 CLUE** and if you want to take the **[MAP OF THE TUNNELS]** with you, record it on your Character Sheet.

Turn to **239**.

72

Taking the **[SEA GOLD]** from your pack, you wave it at the fish-thing, immediately catching its attention. Breaking off its attack, it watches you – or rather the lustrous piece of metal you are holding in your hand – with opaque eyes.

"You want this?" You jerk your hand first one way then the other, the monster's unblinking gaze never once leaving the **[SEA GOLD]**. "Then go fetch!"

You throw the gold as far as you can into the middle of the lake. It lands in the water with a plop and rapidly sinks toward the bottom, although you have no idea how far down that might be.

Hissing angrily, with barely a moment's hesitation, the creature performs an impressive dive into the pool and with one powerful frog-kick of its legs, it disappears in pursuit of the shiny bauble.

Strike the **[SEA GOLD]** from your Character Sheet and take the SECRET: *Gone Fishing*.

Not waiting to see if it comes back, you turn tail yourself and flee from the cave as fast as you can.

Turn to **136**.

73

Seizing the sodden strands of the net, you hoist it into the air and, with a spinning action, hurl it at one of the fish-men. It lands on top of the deep-dweller, which loses its footing under the weight of the net and crumples to the deck, where it lies kicking its legs in frustration.

This leaves you with the two remaining invaders to deal with. You may spend **1 RESOURCE** at the start of each round to add 2 to your total for that round.

Round one: roll two dice and add your **COMBAT**, but then deduct the current doom level. If you have the {**AGILE**} Ability, add 1. If the total is 14 or more, you win the first round.

Round two: roll two dice and add your **COMBAT**. If you have the {**FIGHTER**} Ability, add 1. If you won the first round, add 2. If your total is 15 or more, you win the second round.

If you won the second round, turn to **32**.
If you lost the second round, turn to **53**.

Your eye is drawn to a shortwave radio standing on a shelf behind the counter that seems as oddly out of place as the shop's proprietor.

Following your gaze, still smiling, the young man says, "That's not for sale, I'm afraid."

"What do you have it for, then?" you ask.

"So I can communicate with ships around Innsmouth Harbor and beyond. I sometimes pick up boats as far away as Cape Ann or Massachusetts Bay."

If you want to ask the shopkeeper if he can try contacting a ship now, turn to **64**.
If you would rather spend some time looking at those things he does have for sale, turn to **94**.

When the two of you arrive at the hotel, bedraggled and wet, the elderly gentleman behind the reception desk says nothing by way of a greeting, but doesn't hide the fact he is watching you as you cross the lobby and then climb the stairs to the top floor.

As soon as you are inside Room #428 once more, Dr Addison closes the door and locks it, using the key that she still has about her person.

"So, can we talk about what's going on here?" you demand as she fusses over the papers that are strewn around her room. It looks like someone else has been in here since you left.

"Shhh! Keep your voice down!" she hisses. "You don't know who might be listening."

"Very well," you reply, lowering your voice. "The advert said you wanted help finding the wreck of a pirate ship that sank off the Innsmouth coast seventy years ago."

Dr Addison doesn't look up as she continues to rifle through the papers on the small table. "Correct."

"'Not for the faint-hearted. Experience working at sea an advantage but not essential,'" you say, quoting from the advert itself.

"Also correct."

You pause, questions crowding your mind like a school of fish. Originally, you had one question to answer: Where was Dr Addison?

But following your flight from the tidal tunnels you have more questions than you started with. You want answers, but what do you want to ask first?

"Why are we really here?" Turn to **85**.
"What were you doing in the tidal tunnels?" Turn to **95**.
"Who took you prisoner?" Turn to **105**.

76

"May I have the key to Room #428?" you ask the man boldly.

"It is not hotel policy to give out guest room keys," the manager replies, smiling warmly. "I'm sure you understand."

"Yes, but I have arranged to meet a… colleague here," you explain poorly, "in Room #428. She is expecting me."

"Here at the Gilman House Hotel, we take our guests' privacy very seriously," the elderly gentleman says. "Who is your colleague?"

You tell him that her name is Dr Stella Addison, but then he starts to ask you more probing questions about her.

Make a knowledge test. Roll one die and add your **INTELLECT**. Alternatively, you can spend **1 CLUE** to roll two dice instead, add them together, and then add the sum to your total **INTELLECT**. If you have the **{ACADEMIC}** or **{STUDIOUS}** Ability, add 1.

What is the result?

8 or higher: turn to **265**.
7 or less: turn to **245**.

77

"So, what brings you to Innsmouth?" the shopkeeper asks.

You catch yourself before deciding that you have nothing to lose by telling him the truth. "I replied to an ad in the *Arkham*

Advertiser. I'm here to aid a renowned academic in the search for a ship that sank off the coast hereabouts some seventy years ago."

"A shipwreck, you say?" Your words have clearly piqued his interest. "I wonder if it's one I have the logbook for." He indicates the southern wall of the shop with a sweep of his arm. There you see a full bookshelf rammed with myriad leatherbound journals. "Every book on that shelf is a ship's log," he explains. "Many of them belonged to vessels that were abandoned off the coast and I'm told some were mysteriously salvaged from ships that have disappeared altogether. I like to read extracts from them on days when business is less than brisk... which is most days, to be honest."

You have clearly found yourself a local expert. Perhaps Dr Addison has been here too. But if she hasn't, perhaps you could aid her in her search for the lost pirate ship by testing Jack Henderson on the subject now.

To ask Jack if he has encountered Dr Addison, turn to **171**.
To ask him about the lost pirate ship, turn to **181**.
Alternatively, if you would like to take a look at some of the stranger items for sale, turn to **37**.
But if you think it is time to leave the shop, turn to **84**.

As soon as the cultists see the [**CARVED IDOL**], they are driven into a frenzy, giving voice to hideous ululating cries, their eyes burning a bright yellow-gold.

Turn to **116**.

In contrast to the exterior of the building, just like the rest of the interior of the jail you have seen up until this point, the jail's holding cells are well maintained. In fact, they look like they have recently been fitted with new steel bars and sturdy locks.

It is in one of these cells that you now find yourself alone, the two policemen having left you to consider your miserable plight. The cell offers you cold comfort; the bed is a concrete slab, the latrine no more than a bucket, and there is not even a blanket to shield you from the bone-numbing cold.

With nothing else to do, you stare at the whitewashed walls and steel bars as you mull over in your mind the events that have brought you to this point.

Make an observation test. Roll one die and add your **INTELLECT**. You can spend **1 CLUE** to add +1 to the total. What's the result?

Total of 8 or more: turn to **69**.
7 or less: turn to **59**.

80

Your attacker has the high ground and, therefore, the advantage. As he stabs at you again with the boat hook, you twist to avoid its rusty tip, thereby losing your balance on the slippery rocks.

What follows is a moment of scrabbling panic as you grab at anything that might arrest your fall. But with nothing beneath your feet but the cold fog and empty air, even when you manage to grab hold of a ledge, momentum and your own body weight pull you free again and you plummet to the rocks below.

You die on impact, every bone in your body breaking as it is smashed against the boulders at the foot of the cliff.

The End.

81

As you stroll between the shop's numerous stacks, you scan the titles and authors visible on the many book spines. However, they do not appear to be organized in either alphabetical order or by subject matter.

> If you have the {**ARCANE STUDIES**} or {**SECRET RITES**} Ability, turn to **62** at once before reading further.
> If not, but you have the {**SEEKER**}, {**ACADEMIC**}, or {**STUDIOUS**} Ability, turn to **71**.
> If you have none of these Abilities, turn to **209**.

82

You have never seen a more derelict or uninviting harbor than that of this crumbling fishing town. Wooden planks have rotted away, posts have been sheared off by winter storms, and festering piles of rubbish litter the quayside. No wonder most sea captains choose to unload their cargo at one of the other ports along the coast.

> If you have received a bottle of [**WHISKEY**] since arriving in Innsmouth, turn to **27**.
> If not, turn to **223**.

83

The Gilman House Hotel is a four-story building and the only remaining establishment of its kind in the town. And, like Innsmouth itself, what might once have been considered luxurious is now but a shadow of its former self; its walls are covered with faded, peeling yellow paint while the pair of cupolas that adorn its roof, and help it stand out against the skyline of the decaying town, are in a sorry state of disrepair. But nonetheless, this is where Dr Addison is staying and where you agreed to meet her.

The hotel lobby is as shabby as the exterior façade and there is only one member of staff on duty, as far as you can tell. He is an elderly man who, you are relieved to see, does not have the curious "Innsmouth look" that so many of the local populace appear to share.

You take a seat on a moldering couch and wait for Dr Addison to arrive for your meeting. The old man behind the desk doesn't say anything but his silent stare keeps seeking you out.

However, two o'clock comes and goes with no sign of the academic making an appearance. When the clock on the wall reads quarter past you start to wonder if she has forgotten your appointment, and when it is half past the hour your irritation at being forgotten has turned to a simmering anger.

What do you want to do?

Stay where you are in the hope that Dr Addison will eventually make an appearance: turn to **143**.
Go to Dr Addsion's room and see if she is there: turn to **233**.

84

Standing outside the curiosity shop once more, staring at the boarded-up buildings before you, you ruminate on what you have learned about this moldering seaside town and the location of the missing doctor. Spend either **1 CLUE** or **1 RESOURCE** or take +**1 DOOM**.

Choosing somewhere you haven't been already, where do you want to go now?

The Little Bookshop: turn to **91**.
Down to the shore: turn to **126**.
The Innsmouth Harbor: turn to **82**.
The Innsmouth Cannery: turn to **281**.
If there is an alternative location you would like to visit, turn to **170**.

85

"You must know that already," comes Dr Addison's barbed retort.

"Humor me."

"We're here to find the wreck of the Jīn Fēng, or Golden Breeze, flagship of the pirate queen Mèng Yáo."

"But why?" When you consider the dark truths that were revealed to you in the tidal tunnels under Innsmouth, you feel there should be more to her answer than just this.

Dr Addison puts down the papers she's been shuffling.

"The truth is, I am less interested in the wreck itself than the pirate queen's lost treasure."

Of course she is. And there was you thinking that the academic might have been motivated by more than just money.

"Very well," you reply, "but won't the treasure have gone down with the ship?"

"Not according to one legend," Addison counters. "Rumor has it that Mèng Yáo buried a mysterious and highly valuable item somewhere along this stretch of coast, along with a fortune in gold."

"Was this before or after her ship sank?"

"Legend also has it that if this treasure is ever found," Dr Addison goes on, "Mèng Yáo will return from the sea to claim it."

"So, afterwards then. What is this mysterious item?"

"Some sources say it was a magical amulet, others claim it was an ancient totem. But a common element of all the stories is that it came from Atlantis."

What is this preposterous nonsense? Lost pirate gold? Atlantis?

"Sounds like a salty sea dog's tale to me," you snort. "I mean… Atlantis?"

"You may mock, but Atlantis was a once mighty civilization. The people who lived there had a far greater mastery of the esoteric and the arcane than we do today. Some of their mages were so powerful that they even threatened the might of the sea deities, until the cataclysm occurred which saw the tectonic plates shift and the lost continent drowned deep beneath the waves."

"And you believe this... talisman... was created by the Atlanteans?"

"I do. And if we can find it, it will be the most incredibly important archaeological discovery of the decade, if not the century."

Since Dr Addison is in such a talkative mood, what do you want to ask her next?

"What were you doing in the tidal tunnels?" Turn to **95**.
"Who took you prisoner?" Turn to **105**.
If you're done interrogating the academic, turn to **115**.

86

You have heard nothing good about Devil Reef, but then why would you when it has a name like that? But its treacherous black shoals would be just the sort of place that could send a ship to the bottom of the ocean. Dr Addison agrees and so, as soon as she has bundled her research notes into a leather satchel, the two of you head for the harbor. After all, you're going to need a boat to reach the reef.

Devil Reef can just be seen from the breakwater. It appears as a black scar on the horizon.

If you have a [BRASS TELESCOPE] and want to use it to scrutinize the reef, turn to **21**.
If not, turn to **118**.

Snatching up the **[HARPOON]**, you thrust it at your enemies as if it were a spear.

Take +**1 RESOURCE** and +**1 COMBAT**, and record the **[HARPOON]** on your Character Sheet. You may spend **1 RESOURCE** at the start of each round to add 2 to your total for that round.

Round one: roll two dice and add your **COMBAT**, but then deduct the current doom level. If you have the **{AGILE}** Ability, add 1. If the total is 15 or more, you win the first round.

Round two: roll two dice and add your **COMBAT**. If you have the **{FIGHTER}** Ability, add 1. If you won the first round, add 2. If your total is 16 or more, you win the second round.

Round three: roll two dice and add your **COMBAT**. If you have the **{TOUGH}** Ability, add 1. If you won the second round, add 2. If your total is 17 or more, you win the second round.

If you won at least two rounds, turn to **32**.
If you lost two or more rounds, turn to **53**.

The first thug, the one carrying the plank of wood, takes a swing at you with his improvised club, but you are too quick for him. As his blow fails to connect, he stumbles while you dodge out of the way, confronting the second and taking him by surprise. As well as avoiding the thugs' punches, you manage to get in a few deft jabs of your own. Take **+1 COMBAT**.

These troublemakers clearly weren't expecting so much resistance. They stagger backward, pausing to take stock of the situation. One of them has dropped the **[CUDGEL]** he was carrying. If you want to take the **[CUDGEL]**, record it on your Character Sheet and take **+1 RESOURCE**.

Making the most of the opportunity presented by this unexpected lull in the fighting, you hurry away down the dilapidated street. The only sounds you can hear are the splashing of your feet in the puddled ruts between the cobbles and the keening cries of seabirds circling overhead. You cannot hear anything that would suggest you are being pursued by the gang of thugs.

Turn to **36**.

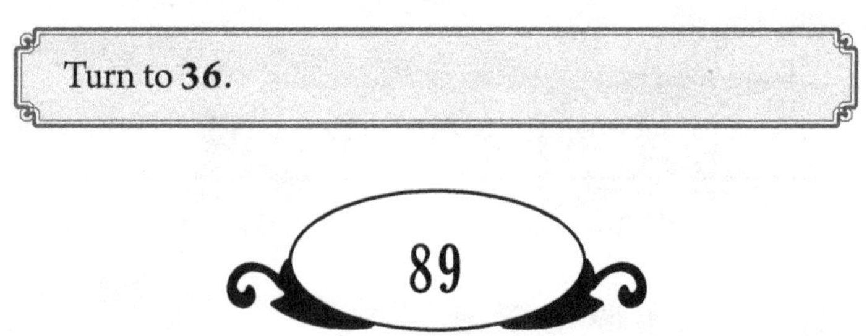

Leaving the two police officers rolling on the floor and doubled up in pain, you flee Innsmouth Jail. Your heart pounding against your ribs, you run down Mill Street, intent on putting as much distance between yourself and any potential pursuit.

You soon find yourself in the warren of streets of the Factory District. The empty windows gaze down upon you like the eyeless sockets of an entire mausoleum of skulls, making you feel increasingly uneasy. Take -**1 SANITY**.

If you have the Weakness **{WATCHED}**, turn to **7**.
If not, turn to **34**.

90

Seemingly against all the odds, you ultimately succeed in sending each of the repulsive, slimy-skinned fish-men back into the waves. Meanwhile, Dr Addison does exactly what you told her to do and keeps the ship on an even keel and level heading, following the dulled beam of the Falcon Point Lighthouse. Take +**1 COMBAT**.

Turn to **174**.

Midtown Innsmouth is an untidy sprawl of condemned structures and ailing businesses, half of which look like they have probably gone out of business already. Amongst this social and civic degradation, The Little Bookshop is a haven of color and light. The warm glow of electric lamps draws you to its orange-painted door, which you push open and enter the shop.

It is everything you hoped it would be, crammed with bookshelves that bow under the weight of the books filling them. Among the overburdened bookcases, comfortable armchairs offer potential purchasers the chance to savor a chapter or two in a relaxed environment without being made to feel obligated to buy anything. The shop's proprietor is a prim, smartly dressed woman with coiffured hair the color of warm leather and a pair of glasses balanced on the end of her nose. Despite her obvious attractiveness, the manner of her dress and the fact she doesn't acknowledge you with even a glance when you enter The Little Bookshop suggest she holds little store by it.

While the rest of Innsmouth malingers under a pall of cold, gray dreariness, The Little Bookshop is a cozy nook where book lovers can while away an hour or two.

Bearing in mind the reason you came here, what do you want to do?

If you want to peruse the shelves, turn to **81**.
If you want to speak with the woman behind the desk, turn to **229**.

92

You uncork one of the heavy bottles and the acrid fumes of the alcohol hit you immediately, making you gasp and your eyes water. But you've come this far, so put the bottle to your lips and take a swig.

It feels like the liquid is burning the inside of your mouth but rather than spit it out, you instinctively swallow. The moonshine then continues to burn its way down your throat, making you cough, before hitting your stomach, rapidly producing an uncomfortable feeling in your chest like heartburn.

However, despite feeling like you are drinking undiluted paint thinner, the burning sensation soon subsides and is replaced by a pleasant warmth that spreads throughout your body to every extremity. Not only that but you feel your resolve strengthening; woe betide anyone who might dare challenge you now!

Take **+1 HEALTH**, **+1 COMBAT**, **+1 WILLPOWER**, and the SECRET: *Dutch Courage.* However, also take **+1 DOOM**.

Choosing something you haven't done already, what do you want to do now?

Take a closer look at the tools that have been left here: turn to **102**.
Leave the gallery and resume your search: turn to **122**.

93

What do you want to pull from your pack and brandish before the advancing cultists of the Esoteric Order of Dagon?

A [CARVED IDOL], if you have one: turn to **78**.
An [OCTOPUS CROWN], if you have such a thing: turn to **58**.
Some [SEA GOLD], if you have any: turn to **44**.
If you have none of these items, turn to **106**.

94

"Let me know if there's anything I can help you with," the man repeats as you take in the eclectic mix of items that are for sale in Henderson's Oddities. "After all, it's my name that's above the door: HENDERSON'S ODDITIES. Jack Henderson, at your service."

Oddities is the right word. As well as the kind of maritime

tools and charts the skipper of a fishing trawler would find useful, there are some far stranger objects. These range from curious pagan deities carved from teak, objets d'art cast from a mysterious whitish-gold metal, and other objects that you cannot begin to fathom what reason they were created for in the first place.

If you want to take a closer look at the maritime tools that are for sale, turn to **104**.
If you want to examine the more esoteric artifacts, turn to **37**.
If you want to ask the proprietor if he has encountered Dr Addison, turn to **171**.
But if you are done here and merely want to leave the curiosity shop, turn to **84**.

"I was searching for the lost treasure of Mèng Yáo," Dr Addison admits. "Considering the clues I had found, I was sure it was buried down there somewhere."

"But it wasn't."

"You don't know that," Dr Addison snaps. "It could still be down there. I just haven't found the right spot yet."

Dr Stella Addison is clearly a formidable individual and not to be underestimated, but that doesn't mean she is right regarding the location of the lost treasure.

"Why were you so sure it was in the tunnels?" you challenge the academic.

"I thought some of the locals might have recovered it and hidden it there. After all, all sorts of things are hidden down there, not just bootlegger stills."

Her mention of "the locals" takes your mind back to the condition she was in when you found her.

If you want to ask who tied her up and left her down there, turn to **105**.
If you are done with asking questions, turn to **115**.

96

Something like concern seizes the hotelier's slack features and he addresses you for the first time since you entered the establishment. "I had better check it out," he says. "If you will excuse me..."

As soon as he quits his post, you lift the counter hatch and sneak behind the desk. You find the key you are looking for and lift it from the rack. Key in hand, you hurry back upstairs to the top floor. Once there, you insert it into the lock and hear a satisfying click as you give it a turn.

Turn to **235**.

97

You hand responsibility for keeping the boat on course for Falcon Point over to Dr Addison, telling her to steer straight for the beacon of light that is intermittently visible to the south through the swirling fog.

Exiting the wheelhouse, as the vessel is tossed about by the unforgiving waves and a third fish-man pokes its ugly head over the side, you look for something on the deck to help you combat your uninvited guests.

But then again, perhaps you are already in possession of something that might give you power over the fish-men.

What do you want to do?

Grab something from the deck: turn to **158**.
Grab something from your pack: turn to **188**.

98

You fight to suppress the rising panic that threatens to overwhelm you as the mutated creature – whatever it is! – tightens its hold still further. Eventually you kick yourself free but your battle with the grotesque catch of the day has cost you.

You have heard rumors that fishing vessels operating off the Innsmouth coast find things in their nets far stranger than anglerfish and spider crabs, things with disturbingly human-seeming faces and tentacled creatures that are neither squid nor octopus that are found nowhere else. But when mariner tales like that are revealed to be true, it makes you wonder what other impossible stories you've heard are actually fact.

Take -1 **HEALTH**, -1 **SANITY**, and the SECRET: *Catch of the Day.*

Hurrying to the far end of the unloading bay you find an unlocked door and waste no time in passing through it into the Cannery proper.

Turn to **139**.

99

Being very careful where you step, fully aware that if you were to trip and fall it could end in disaster, you head toward the edge of the cliff. After all, the treasure you seek is hidden in a cave under Falcon Point, or so you believe.

You soon find yourself standing right at the edge of the precipice, the cliff face curving away beneath you in a vertiginous drop. However, it is not a sheer cliff; there is a precarious way down, lacking anything that would arrest your fall should you slip, such as a handrail, or even a few iron rungs hammered into the rock.

"There's nothing else for it," Dr Addison says, also considering the dizzying descent. "If we're going to recover Mèng Yáo's booty, we are going to have to tackle that path."

So you set off, but with Dr Addison leading the way down. It takes a great deal of concentration as you consider each step cautiously before committing to it.

A noise, like the crunch of gravel, has you turning in time to see a man wearing a waxed raincoat and sou'wester hat. Tangles of hair have escaped from under the hat to gather on his chin as a scraggly beard.

The beam of the lighthouse sweeps over your position, exposing him to the light, and in that snapshot moment you take in everything.

Clutched in his hands is a boat hook, which he is thrusting in your direction. Clearly his intention is to send you plummeting to your death on the rocks far below. But that is not the worst thing you see in that split second of stark luminescence. The hands holding the shaft of the boat hook appear to be linked by webs of skin and the fingernails are more like sharpened claws. But there is still something else worse than that.

The man's untidy hair frames a face that has been subjected to some dreadful disease or mutation. The skin is covered in malformed scales, while his eyes are like two pearls, glistening and devoid of either pupil or iris. His blunt nose appears to be receding into his face, while his black-lipped mouth is crammed with irregular, needle-like teeth.

Take the SECRET: *Odd Fish.*

Another stabbing thrust of the boat hook shakes you from your appalled reverie. Despite your precarious position, you have no choice but to defend yourself or you will meet your end here. You may spend **1 RESOURCE** at the start of each round to add 2 to your total for that round.

Round one: roll two dice and add your **COMBAT**. If you have the **{AGILE}** Ability, add 1. If you have the Weakness **{FEAR OF HEIGHTS}**, deduct 2. If the total is 15 or more, you win the first round.

Round two: roll two dice and add your **COMBAT**. If you won the first round, add 2. If you have the **{AGILE}** Ability, add 1. If you have the Weakness **{FEAR OF HEIGHTS}**, deduct 2. If you won the first round, add 1. If your total is 16 or more, you win the second round.

If you won the second round, turn to **66**.
If you lost the second round, turn to **80**.

It is no good. What is your mind compared to the will of Father Dagon?

Unable to bear the pressure anymore, you collapse, physically as well as mentally, dropping to your knees on the cold stones of the foreshore in a swoon.

You may be unconscious, but you are still breathing when the horrors offer you up as a living sacrifice to their patriarch deity.

Defiant to the last, you tried your best, but in the end, it still was not enough.

Take the SECRET: *Lord Dagon.*

Final score: 1 star.

The End.

101

Opening the door, you poke your head through and glance left and right, but can see no sign of whoever – or whatever – it was that you are convinced you heard outside the room. However, you cannot shake the feeling that your presence in the town has been noted and your actions are being observed from afar. Take the Weakness {**PARANOID**}.

Turn to **164**.

102

There are several items that could prove useful, if only as improvised weapons if you unexpectedly find yourself in a tight spot. There is a [**SCREWDRIVER**], a [**WOODEN MALLET**], and the aforementioned coil of rough hemp [**ROPE**].

Record any of the items you want to take on your Character Sheet. For each one you take you may also take **+1 RESOURCE**.

When you are done, choosing something you haven't tried already, what do you want to do next?

Sample some of the moonshine: turn to **92**.
Leave the still and resume your exploration of the tidal tunnels: turn to **122**.

103

"I know that Dr Addison had been studying the times of the tides around Innsmouth," you tell Ropes. "I was supposed to meet her at the Gilman House Hotel, but she never showed. I managed to gain entry to her room" – at this comment, the deputy constable raises a suspicious eyebrow – "and I found a book of tide times and her diary."

"Did the diary give you any idea where she might have gone?" the police officer asks.

"The only thing written in it that might be relevant were the names of two locations: 'Tidal Tunnels' and 'The Little Bookshop.'"

"So now we know why she had the book of tide times," Ropes says. "There are hidden entrances to the sea caves and the network of tunnels connecting them along the coast, but they are only revealed at low tide. Some of them run all the way into town. But it's easy to get lost down there, and you don't want to find yourself stuck in that twisting labyrinth when high tide comes."

Take **+2 CLUES** but also take the Weakness **{WATCHED}**.

Turn to **213**.

Giving the various sextants, compasses and other navigational tools only the most cursory of glances, you feel drawn to a chart of the waters off the seaport of Innsmouth. It has been annotated by a scratchy hand. Where a channel between a shoal of submerged rocks is shown, the annotator has written the words, "Don't set pots here," and in the empty space the original cartographer left to the east of Devil Reef, the same hand has scrawled, "Atlantis?"

However, as well as these curious inscriptions, the one who annotated the chart has also marked the coastline and shallower waters with various crosses, each of which either has a date written next to it, or what you take to be the name of a ship, and in some cases both.

"I've spent a fair few hours studying that one myself," the shop's proprietor says, appearing at your shoulder, "but I'm not averse to parting with it for the right price."

Henderson is prepared to exchange the [TREASURE HUNTER'S CHART] for something else desirable at a cost of 1 resource.

If you want to make the swap, turn to **124**.
If you would prefer not to, turn to 77.

"Let's just say that Innsmouth folk guard their privacy jealously. They certainly don't like outsiders sticking their oar in. Not that they would appreciate the true value of what the pirate queen brought back from the South China Sea, the inbred ignoramuses."

"But if that was the case, wouldn't they try to drive you out of town after maybe giving you a beating first? Why tie you up and keep you prisoner? Was someone hoping to collect a ransom for your safe return?"

Dr Addison gives a snort of derision but doesn't say anything to contradict you. Take +**1 CLUE**.

"Now, if you're done asking questions, perhaps we can formulate a plan with regard to what we need to do next," she states.

Turn to **115**.

Surrounded now as you are on all sides, you charge the closing cultists directly in front of you, hoping to barge your way past them before they can seize hold of you.

Make a flight test. Roll one die and add your **COMBAT**, but then deduct the current doom level. Alternatively, you may spend **1 RESOURCE** to roll two dice instead, pick the highest, and then add your **COMBAT**. If you have the **{AGILE}** Ability, add 1. What's the result?

Total of 8 or more: turn to **274**.
7 or less: turn to **116**.

Innsmouth is surrounded by marshes and creeks that help to isolate it from the rest of the country roundabouts. Before embarking on your trip, you did a little digging into the town's history and discovered that it was considered something of a backwater even before a strange plague struck the town in 1846 which claimed the lives of half of its residents. Since then, the town's decline has steadily worsened and even accelerated in recent years.

You can see this for yourself now, and it applies not only to the houses and factories of the place but extends to the state of its roads, including that of the coastal highway that is the only route in and out of the town by car. Not that you arrive by car, making use of the bus service that runs from Arkham to Innsmouth twice a day instead. You sit by a dirt-smeared window with your pack on your lap, in which you have some things that may prove of use while you are in town. Take +2 resources.

The bus is driven by a man called Joe Sargent and, as it rattles along the ill-kept road toward the fishing port, you find yourself morbidly fascinated by his appearance. He has stooped shoulders and a narrow head that is almost hairless. There are deep creases in the sides of his neck that make him appear older than you think he really is, but it is his bulging, watery eyes, long, thick lips, and gray, scabrous cheeks that unsettle you the most. You are glad when the bus pulls up in the Town Square, all too ready to disembark. Take **-1 SANITY.**

You agreed to meet Dr Addison at the Gilman House Hotel at 2:00PM but it is barely noon now, although heavy cloud cover hides the sun from view and the breeze blowing in from the sea is bitingly cold. As if on cue, your belly growls, reminding you that you haven't eaten anything since breakfast several hours ago.

On the other side of the square is the First National Grocery where you could acquire something to eat. Alternatively, you could see if there is a local café somewhere nearby, where they might be serving lunch. There is a signpost pointing the way to the hotel.

What do you want to do?

Enter the First National Grocery: turn to **160**.
Go in search of a café or similar: turn to **128**.
Make your way to the hotel and wait for Dr Addison there: turn to **83**.

You can't shake the feeling that something sinister has befallen Dr Addison and you need help finding her. And for that help, you are going to rely on local law enforcement.

Due in part to the town's general decline, but particularly thanks to the collapse of any public infrastructure, Innsmouth does not have a police station. Instead, as you soon discover, the local police operate out of the town jail.

The building's exterior is as shabby and neglected as any other civic building you have come across since arriving in Innsmouth, but upon passing over its threshold, you are surprised by how well maintained it is inside.

According to the name plaque on the counter, the officer slouched behind it is one Deputy Constable Carey Ropes. As you enter the jail, he looks up at you, almost begrudgingly. He doesn't say anything but waits for you to speak first.

Taking a deep breath, you say, "I want to report a missing person."

If you have the {**DETECTIVE**} or {**POLICE**} Ability, turn to **168**.
If you have the {**CRIMINAL**} Weakness, or the {**ROGUE**} Ability, turn to **273**.
If you have none of these, turn to **148**.

It doesn't matter what excuse you come up with, these unthinking dullards won't be having any of it.

"Look, sling your hook!" the talkative one says, making his feelings plain.

Considering where you are and the regular comings and goings of the workers, even if you could get the better of the goons in a fight, you would soon find yourself overwhelmed by the sheer weight of their numbers and dragged down to the jail, if you were lucky. If not, chances are you would end up in the harbor as food for the fishes with a heavy iron chain wrapped around your ankles.

You get the feeling that wherever you go in the immediate future, these goons, or friends of theirs, are going to be keeping a close eye on you, so it would also be unwise to try to find another way into the Cannery. Take the Weakness **{WATCHED}**.

Turn to **28**.

Turning the key sharply, you yank open the door and the hotel manager stumbles into the room. Totally taken by surprise, he gives you a look of open-mouthed bewilderment but does not see the blow that sends him staggering across the room to land in a heap under the window.

But there are also two of the townsfolk standing in the corridor. Both display the unsettling "Innsmouth look" that is so familiar to you now, and have come prepared: they are carrying bludgeons, in case you put up any resistance. But you are determined to escape this twisted town and will not let two inbred locals stop you.

You may spend **1 RESOURCE** at the start of each round to add 2 to your total for that round – if you have the **RESOURCE** to spend, that is.

Round one: roll two dice and add your **COMBAT** and your **WILLPOWER**. If you have the **{SURVIVOR}** Ability, add 1. If the total is 14 or more, you win the first round.

Round two: roll two dice and add your **COMBAT** and your **WILLPOWER**. If you have the **{TOUGH}** Ability, add 1. If you won the first round, add 2. If your total is 15 or more, you win the second round.

If you won the second round, turn to **120**.
If you lost the second round, turn to **130**.

As you are perusing the papers, you hear the sound of shuffling footsteps again, and then the rattle of somebody trying the door. Fear prevents you from calling out to ask if it is Dr Addison; she would have her own key, surely. And besides, you get the eerie instinctual sensation that whatever is making those shuffling footsteps is not fully human.

Before you can formulate an escape plan, the door opens and you see the silhouettes of several people standing in the passageway. The corridor is in darkness and you cannot discern the expressions of the people standing there, but you are all too aware of their rasping breathing and the rank smell that accompanies them, like dead fish washed up and left to rot on the seashore.

You turn away in horror and cross the room opposite them in a single bound, intending to throw yourself out of the window to get away. As you pull up the sash, you feel strong hands grab your shoulders and then something heavy and hard strikes you between your shoulder blades.

There is a moment of sharp pain followed by cold oblivion. Take -**2 HEALTH**.

Roll one die and deduct 1 if you have the **{SURVIVOR}** or **{TOUGH}** Ability.

If the total is equal to or less than your **HEALTH**, turn to **298**.
If the total is greater than your **HEALTH**, turn to **13**.

112

Taking hold of one of the large barrels, you pull it down with a great grunt of effort. You then do the same with each of the great coppers, your muscles straining as you do so. The chamber reverberates with the crash of metalwork, and it is some time before the ringing noise dies down. However, it will take far longer – many hours, if not days – for the bootleggers to repair the damage you have done in what was less than a minute of frenzied activity. You only hope nobody was around to hear your destruction of the still.

Take -1 **DOOM**, unless you have the Weakness {**PARANOID**}, in which case do not alter the current doom rating.

Your work here done, there is nothing to be gained by hanging around, so you set off once more, wondering when, or even if, you will find Dr Addison.

Turn to **136**.

113

Despite the chill in the air, you feel beads of sweat breaking out on your forehead. You grit your teeth against the pain manifesting within your mind as you resist the mental torment produced by the mere presence of the fish-god.

Make a resistance test. Roll one die, add your **WILLPOWER** and your **SANITY**. You may spend **1 RESOURCE** to roll two dice and pick the highest. What's the result?

> Total of 10 or more: turn to **291**.
> 9 or less: turn to **100**.

114

Not being familiar with the layout of the town, you do your best to determine where the Gilman House Hotel is likely to be located and navigate Innsmouth's derelict streets accordingly. However, it is not an easy task since they are in such a poor state of repair, particularly those close to the sea. One telling sign is that you cannot see many completely intact windows; most are curtained with filthy rags, or boarded up, or empty of glass or shutters of any kind. But you will not be deterred. After all, you have come this far...

Make a navigation test. Roll one die and add your **INTELLECT**. Alternatively, you may spend **1 CLUE** to instead roll two dice instead, add them together, and then add the sum to your **INTELLECT**. If you have the **{QUICK-WITTED}** Ability, add 1, and if you have the **{SEEKER}** Ability, add 1. What's the result?

Total of 8 or more: turn to **140**.
7 or less: turn to **292**.

Dr Addison quickly summarizes her reason for visiting Innsmouth and bringing you here too; she is seeking the wreck of the Golden Breeze – a Chinese junk belonging to the pirate queen Mèng Yáo – but more specifically the mysterious artifact that was rumored to have been on board. However, unpleasant elements among the local populace are onto her and appear set on preventing her from finding the treasure, and they are not above using physical force to get what they want. And who's to say they wouldn't be prepared to go further than merely tying someone up?

"I need someone to watch my back," she concludes. "And help with the heavy lifting."

Even though Dr Addison's advertisement in the *Arkham Advertiser* expressly stated you could expect hazardous working conditions and that the constant threat of danger was guaranteed, the reality and truth of that statement is overwhelming.

As far as you can see, you have two options open to you. You can either press on with the search for the lost treasure of the Golden Breeze, or you can get out of town! So, what's it to be?

To tell Dr Addison you're in this to the bitter end, turn to **153**.
To tell the academic you should leave Innsmouth while you still can, turn to **135**.

Giving voice to your dread and anger in one great, bloodcurdling howl, you lash out at the cultists as they come for you. But despite your spirited attack, there are too many of them and you are soon overwhelmed.

Clearly seeing no point in putting off any longer what they had planned for you, the cultists carry you to another chamber, at the center of which stands an altar of black rock. By the humming electric lights illuminating the hall, you can see rusty stains on the surface of the stone.

Four of the cultists stretch you over the altar stone, each holding one of your limbs, and their priest, wearing a golden crown that looks like an octopus wrapped around his hairless head, steps forward to make the sacrifice to Father Dagon.

The End.

You move at a trot and in no time you are jogging along the quay to where your boat is, thankfully, still moored. Leaping from the quay onto the deck, you prepare to cast off as Dr Addison climbs aboard, demonstrating less confidence around seagoing vessels.

In no time at all, your boat is heading for the mouth of the harbor, the smoky exhaust fumes from its chugging engine merging with the fog. Passing the end of the breakwater, you make out the ruins of the lighthouse that stand there through the miasma. The internal parts of the structure clearly collapsed a long time ago and its lamp hasn't guided ships in and out of the harbor for many a year.

Beyond the calm waters of the harbor, you join the churning swell of the Atlantic and set a course for Falcon Point. Due to the encroaching, green-tinged fog, you are forced to stay close to the shore.

A lighthouse stands atop Falcon Point too, different from the ruined Innsmouth lighthouse, so you use a combination of your ship's compass, the occasional landmark that materializes from the murk, and the guiding beam of the lighthouse that is just visible despite the dense fog.

But before you reach Falcon Point, you pass the black spur of half-submerged rock known locally as Devil Reef. And it is not long after passing this notorious landmark that, from your place inside the wheelhouse, you hear a thud reverberating through the hull of the ship. Dr Addison shoots you an anxious glance.

It is the sort of sound you would expect to hear if the boat had collided with something, but there was no accompanying lurch and yaw to port or starboard. Did something hit the ship from below?

Your unspoken question is answered moments later when a webbed hand reaches over the port bow of the ship, followed by another, and then a glistening domed head.

Someone – or rather something! – is trying to climb on board. And out here, in such choppy conditions, this close to nightfall and in the midst of the worst fog you have ever known, you are certain that it isn't a sailor from another vessel who's fallen overboard and needs rescuing. It can only be something that has risen from the ocean depths to challenge you.

Take the SECRET: *In Deep Water.*

Hearing a scratching sound from the other side of the ship, you snap your head round and see something else, the color of an eel, attempting to slither its way over the gunwale.

One of you is going to need to do something about repelling the boarders, but someone also needs to maintain the boat's course in what are less than ideal sea conditions.

If you want to remain at the wheel and direct Dr Addison to deal with the creatures that are boarding the boat, turn to **138**.

If you want to tell Dr Addison to take the wheel, freeing you up to deal with your unwelcome visitors, turn to **97**.

You will get a better view of the reef when you have crossed the sea to reach it. But to do that you are going to need a boat.

If you have the {**SAILOR**} Ability, turn to **131**.
If not, turn to **146**.

"I was just wondering how an enterprising captain would go about supplying the cannery," you say, coming up with what you hope sounds like a convincing excuse on the spur of the moment.

The goons exchange suspicious glances until the one who first spoke says, "Follow me," and turns to enter the cannery.

If you want to follow him inside, turn to **129**.
If you have had a change of heart and would rather make your excuses and leave, turn to **109**.

Leaving the two heavies doubled up on the floor, groaning in agony, you and Dr Addison grab what you need and flee Room #428.

Descending the steps from the lobby, you hurry back to the Town Square, your eyes seeking out the bus stop, but there is no bus there. You must get out of town, and fast. Bearing in mind that where you ran into trouble was north of the Manuxet River, your surest ways out of Innsmouth have to be to the south along the coast road to Arkham, or by sea via the harbor.

Looking east in the direction of the harbor, you are horrified to see a thick sea fog rolling in from the ocean. Dusk is already falling, but the advancing black-and-green-tinged fog is smothering everything within the fishing town and even dimming the streetlamps that are just coming on.

"Come on!" snaps Dr Addison. "We cannot delay any longer. We can't let a little fog delay us." And so, you begin to make your way out of town.

However, as the fog first blurs and then absorbs the surrounding buildings, thereby robbing you of any useful landmarks and stealing away your natural sense of direction, you become aware of other things moving within the murk. You spot one and, soon after, a second and a third. Before long, you come to the chilling realization that you are surrounded by shadowy figures.

The lumpen forms appear to be human, or at least humanoid, walking upright on two legs, but you strain to make out any more details. But it is the strange cries echoing through the fog that raises both your heart rate and the hackles on the back of your neck.

You can hear an amphibian croaking, an indefinable hooting, and unintelligible gibbering. And then there are the voices, although they sound like they are coming from throats clogged with phlegm and not in any language you can understand.

You keep close to Dr Addison but out here on the streets of the decaying fishing town, in the clammy grip of the all-enveloping miasma, you feel a creeping sense of dread and a cold knot of fear forms in the pit of your stomach. Then all your worst fears come to fruition as the figures close in around you and you see their hairless, slack-jawed faces and watery, wide-set eyes, and you know then that you will never escape this cursed town. You feel slimy hands seize you and a split second later something hits you across the back of the head and you lose consciousness. Take -**1 HEALTH**.

Roll one die and deduct 1 if you have the **{SURVIVOR}** or **{TOUGH}** Ability.

If the total is equal to or less than your **HEALTH**, turn to **298**.
If the total is greater than your **HEALTH**, turn to **13**.

You feel slightly uncomfortable reading the doctor's diary, as if you are invading her privacy by doing so. But needs must...

Finding today's date, you see "2:00PM" written in pencil and your initials next to it. There are no other appointments recorded in the diary for this week. However, scribbled across the bottom of the page is the following note:

Tidal Tunnels under town – entrance exposed at low tide. Link to The Little Bookshop?

Having already crossed a line by reading **[DR ADDISON'S DIARY]**, you decide to cross another one and take the diary with you.

A sudden noise outside the room makes you start. It sounded like something being dragged along the hallway outside. You freeze, barely daring to breathe, as the shuffling footsteps move away along the corridor.

What do you want to do now?

Continue to examine the papers on the table: turn to **111**.
Leave the hotel without delay and go in search of Dr Addison: turn to **101**.

122

You are about to leave the chamber when you are filled with a sudden destructive urge. Stills like this one are established by bootleggers so they can flout the Prohibition laws and produce their illegal alcohol right under the noses of the authorities.

> If you want to do what you can to dismantle the still before you leave the cave, turn to **112**.
> If you don't want to risk attracting the attention of any bootleggers who might be down here in the tidal tunnels with you, turn to **136**.

123

"I know that Dr Addison had been studying the times of the tides around Innsmouth," you tell Ropes. "I was supposed to meet her at the Gilman House Hotel, but she never showed. I managed to gain entry to her room" – at this remark the deputy constable raises an eyebrow – "and I found a book of tide times and a copy of the *Innsmouth Tribune* among her possessions. The newspaper was folded open on an article about seismic activity that has been recorded in the area and another concerning the new Cannery."

"Ah yes," says Ropes, "another venture undertaken by the beneficent Marsh family. Old Man Marsh and his bloodline have done a lot for this town; more than you'll ever know. But what about the book of tide times? Why do you think she had that in her room?"

Deciding you're not going to get anywhere if you're dishonest with the policeman, you say, "She was searching for a pirate ship wreck, but I very much doubt that would be revealed at low tide."

"I wouldn't know about that," says the deputy constable, "but I do know what is revealed at low tide – the tidal tunnels, of course." The police officer smiles smugly. "They run from the shore right under the town. But it's easy to get lost down there, and you don't want to find yourself stuck in that half-flooded labyrinth at high tide."

Take +1 **CLUE** but also take the Weakness **{WATCHED}**.

Turn to **213**.

124

You make the exchange. Take -1 **RESOURCE** and +1 **CLUE**, and then add the **[TREASURE HUNTER'S CHART]** to your Character Sheet.

"Perhaps I can interest you in this," Henderson says, taking a gleaming, collapsable brass telescope down from another shelf. "If you're planning on going treasure hunting with that chart, it could prove invaluable. I'm prepared to part with this on similar terms."

If you want to, and have the wherewithal to do so, the shopkeeper will exchange the **[BRASS TELESCOPE]** for **2 RESOURCES**.

Once you are done, turn to **77**.

125

"I believe the treasure is buried beneath Falcon Point," you tell Dr Addison, and a look of astonished wonder creeps over her face.

"Of course!" she exclaims delightedly. "I see it now. How could I have been so foolish to think it was in the tidal tunnels? Well, now we know where it is, we mustn't delay. We must set off straight away."

Dr Addison bundles her most precious possessions – her research notes – into a leather satchel and then the two of you hurry down the stairs to the lobby and leave the Gilman House Hotel.

"Falcon Point lies several miles south along the coast from here," Dr Addison muses, surveying the Town Square and its solitary bus stop.

You can't afford to hang around, not if you don't want to run into Dr Addison's captors again. Considering all your options, you look east, in the direction of the harbor, and are perturbed to see a thick sea fog rolling in off the Atlantic Ocean. Dusk is starting to spread its mantle across the land, but the advancing fog is smothering everything within the fishing town, even dimming the glowing streetlamps that are just coming on.

If you have the {**SAILOR**} Ability, turn to **24**.
If not, turn to **224**.

North, beyond the bay and the breakwater, you make your way down to the sandy shoreline. It is as unwelcoming as anywhere in Innsmouth, with jagged rocks jutting from the soft sand like the fangs of some long-dead sea monster.

All manner of rubbish has washed up on the beach, including several dead fish. At least, you think they are fish. You dare not let your gaze linger upon them for too long. They are unlike any sea creatures you have seen before.

Take the SECRET: *I Do Like to be Beside the Seaside.*

Proceeding farther along the beach you come to a place where the land is bounded by rugged cliffs. You get the impression that some of the crevices and inlets could lead to caves, but any openings there may be are currently inaccessible due to the current sea level.

There are rock pools along this stretch of shore. Hearing a frantic splash, you realize that something has become trapped in one of them by the receding tide.

If you want to investigate, turn to **297**.
If you think you have seen enough of this desolate beach, turn to **28**.

127

There are three of them and only one of you. All three have the hulking build of fishermen, used to hauling in heavy nets and battling the might of the sea. If you are to have any hope of overcoming them, you are going to have to stay light on your feet and not get trapped into taking on more than one of them at a time.

You may spend **1 RESOURCE** at the start of each round to add 2 to your total for that round.

Round one: roll two dice and add your **COMBAT**. If you have the **{FIGHTER}** or **{ROGUE}** Ability, add 1. If the total is 10 or more, you win the first round.

Round two: roll two dice and add your **COMBAT**. If you have the **{FIGHTER}** or **{ROGUE}** Ability, add 1. If you won the first round, add 1. If your total is 11 or more, you win the second round.

Round three: roll two dice and add your **COMBAT**. If you have the **{FIGHTER}** or **{ROGUE}** Ability, add 1. If you have the **{TOUGH}** Ability, you may also add 1. And if you won the second round, add 2. If your total is 12 or more, you win the third round.

If you won at least two rounds, turn to **88**.
If you lost at least two rounds, turn to **16**.

128

The Town Square is bordered to the north by the Manuxet River. Keeping this to one side of you, you set off in search of somewhere to have some lunch, to placate your grumbling belly.

> If you have the Weakness
> {**TAINTED LINEAGE**}, turn to **290**.
> If not, turn to **292**.

129

Inside, the cannery is dimly lit and any windows you see are covered with tattered swags of hessian or smeared with dirt, so that they let in only the slightest amount of muted light from outside. The burly local leads you through the factory and then opens an unremarkable wooden door. He admits you to a small room and tells you, "Wait here."

As the door closes behind him, you take in your surroundings. The room is furnished with nothing more than two chairs and a small table. What takes up most of the space are boxes labelled "The Innsmouth Cannery." One of the boxes is open and you can see tins of sardines packed in like… well… sardines.

You don't know where the worker went but as time passes you realize you don't really want to wait around to find out. You're here to learn what has happened Dr Addison, so it would make more sense to take a look around the cannery without being accompanied by anybody who is actually employed here.

However, it's been some time since you arrived in Innsmouth, and you can feel your stomach knotting with hunger. Perhaps it would be wise to make the most of the situation and help yourself to a tin of sardines to replenish your strength.

If you want to leave the room and begin your search straightaway, turn to **139**.
If you want to sample some of the sardines first, turn to **149**.

The heavies are too strong for you, and you are left lying on the floor of the hotel, wincing as you nurse your bruised ribs. Having subdued you, they soon get the better of Dr Addison as well.

As you are wondering what will happen to you now, more heavyset men enter the room and drag you to your feet. As they manhandle you toward the stairs, you make one last effort to break free of their clutches. But you are exhausted and your attempt proves futile.

However, while you don't achieve your aim of breaking free, it does motivate the thugs to do something about your continued struggling. Something hard connects with the back of your skull and you lose consciousness immediately. Take -**2 HEALTH**.

Roll one die and deduct 1 if you have the **{SURVIVOR}** or **{TOUGH}** Ability.

If the total is equal to or less than your **HEALTH**, turn to **298**.
If the total is greater than your **HEALTH**, turn to **13**.

You make your way along the quay to where your boat is moored. Leaping from the harborside onto the deck, you prepare for the off as Dr Addison climbs aboard, demonstrating less confidence around seagoing vessels.

In no time at all, your boat is heading for the mouth of the harbor, the smoky exhaust fumes from its chugging engine merging with the fog. Passing the end of the breakwater, you see the ruins of the Innsmouth Lighthouse that stand there; the internal parts of the structure clearly collapsed a long time ago and its lamp hasn't guided ships in and out of the harbor for many a year.

Beyond the calm waters of the harbor, you join the churning swell of the Atlantic and steer your vessel toward Devil Reef.

As you close in on the mysterious landmark, you hear a thud that reverberates through the hull of the ship. Dr Addison shoots you an anxious look.

It is the sort of sound you would expect to hear if the boat had run aground on the half-submerged shoals, but there was no accompanying lurch and yaw to port or starboard. Did something else collide with the ship from below?

Your unspoken question is answered moments later, when a webbed hand reaches over the port bow of the ship, followed by another, and then a glistening domed head. Something is trying to climb on board.

Hearing a scratching sound from the other side of the ship, you snap your head round and see something else, the color of an eel, attempting to slither its way over the gunwale.

Dr Addison rushes out of the wheelhouse, a boat hook in hand, and lashes out with it to drive off the horrors. But more are climbing on board with every passing moment. You have invaded their territory and for that you will pay the ultimate price.

Dr Addison is a scholar and not a fighter, and she soon falls foul of the grotesque boarding party. As she flails at one of the fish-men with the hooked pole, the creature seizes her improvised weapon and yanks it from her grasp. In the next moment, another of the creatures leaps on her from the gunwale, like some enormous toad.

You watch all of this through the spray-drenched windows of the wheelhouse, unable to do anything to help the wretched woman. But her ultimate fate remains a mystery to you as more of the fish-people board your boat, forcing their way into the wheelhouse. You do your best to defend yourself, but it is already too late.

You and Dr Addison will share a watery grave at the bottom of the Atlantic Ocean, while your boat will finally come to rest on the rugged rocks of the Innsmouth shore, destined to join the list of unaccounted for wrecks washed up along this stretch of the New England coast.

Take the SECRET: *Between the Devil and the Deep Blue Sea.*

The End.

You check the date and see that the newspaper is two days old. It has been folded so that your eye is drawn to the article at the bottom of the page, which bears the headline "Tremors Shake Innsmouth."

Apparently, some recent seismic disturbance has caused minor damage to property and the town's infrastructure, opening potholes in the coastal road and the like. The epicenter of this activity is thought to be off the coast, however, in the vicinity of Devil Reef, although there have also been reports of tremors as far away as Falcon Point.

A smaller piece on the same page is about the Innsmouth Cannery. According to the article, it hasn't been open long, but the town's fortunes are already looking up because of the money the business is bringing into the town, thanks to the goods it produces being sold all over New England. Considering the derelict state of the town, is this honest journalism or merely a propaganda piece? Take **+1 CLUE** and record the [**INNSMOUTH TRIBUNE**] on your Character Sheet.

A sudden noise outside the room makes you start. It sounded like something being dragged along the hallway outside. You freeze, barely daring to breathe, as the shuffling footsteps move away along the corridor.

What do you want to do now?

Continue to examine the papers on the table: turn to **111**.
Leave the hotel without delay and go in search of Dr Addison: turn to **101**.

133

You remain strong and use the rough walls of the tunnel to pull yourself through it as quickly as possible. Your lungs are starting to burn as the luminescence becomes brighter above you and you surface to find yourself in a large, flooded cavern. The eerily glowing fungi proliferate here, revealing to you a most unsettling scene.

On the far side of the cave, three grotesque figures have been positioned on a broad ledge of dark rock. You cannot tell if they have been carved from the fabric of the cave itself or fashioned elsewhere and transported here.

The central figure is the largest, at over eight feet tall. But the monstrous being it portrays is poised in a crouched hunch. If it were real, the creature would stand over twelve feet when fully upright. It appears simian, or perhaps even humanoid, in its basic body structure, but that has been warped by the addition of monstrous bat wings draped around its body, and an octopus-like creature, sporting far too many rubbery arms in place of a head.

This grotesque "god" is flanked by two smaller statues, but these are still at least six feet tall. Their forms are less well defined and remind you of carvings of deities from Polynesia. Both are clearly supposed to be an amalgam of human and fish, but one has a swollen body and a crown of spines on its malformed head, while the other is leaner and has a distinct fin on top of its elongated skull.

All the statues' features are blurred and distorted, as if from centuries of calcium carbonate-rich water dripping onto them, if not millennia.

Beyond the unholy trinity, you can make out what would appear to be another rocky passageway. You have no idea where it might lead but, despite that, its presence is a blessed relief, and you just want to use the exit to get out of this place as quickly as you can. With your heart now set on this path, you set off across the pool.

Consider the list of Weaknesses and Abilities below. If you have more than one of them, respond to whichever appears first on the list.

If you have the {TAINTED LINEAGE} Weakness, turn to **211**.
If you have the {TROUBLED DREAMS} Weakness, turn to **221**.
If you have the {ARCANE STUDIES} Ability, turn to **231**.
If you have the {ANCIENT LANGUAGES} Ability, turn to **242**.
If you have none of these Weaknesses or Abilities, turn to **252**.

134

Focusing your mind, you snap out of the hypnotic trance the chanting had put you under.

You turn from the statue and regard the people who have gathered in this place to pay their fish-god fealty. They all have the same pallid complexion and slack-faced expressions that are bizarrely reminiscent of the statue behind you. They are all dressed in diaphanous robes of sapphire, turquoise, and emerald.

They reach for you with their hands, the splayed fingers reminding you of starfish, and an involuntary shudder of revulsion passes through you.

You are suddenly possessed by the unshakeable knowledge that you must get out of this place as quickly as you can. After all, it seems clear to you now that the people who worship within this strange temple must be members of the Esoteric Order of Dagon. As such, they must have had a hand in your abduction as well as your imprisonment.

What do you want to do?

Run for it and hope you can evade the cultists' grasping hands: turn to **106**.
Put your trust in your fighting prowess and prepare to battle your way to safety: turn to **116**.
Pull an item from your pack that you think will intimidate the cultists, thereby giving you precious seconds to make your escape: turn to **93**.

"Perhaps you are right," Dr Addsion muses. "They are onto us and therefore our position here is compromised. We should make our escape while we still can and return later when we've had a chance to regroup and gather reinforcements."

That's not quite what you had in mind, but right now you're happy to go along with whatever the academic says if it means you can leave this dying fishing town before sunset. And so, you set off without any further delay.

Make a fate test. Roll one die, and if you have the Weakness **{CURSED}**, deduct 1.

> If the result is equal to or lower than the current doom level, turn to **46**.
> If the result is greater than the current doom level, turn to **26**.

The bioluminescence bathes everything in an unreal turquoise light, making it seem like you are underwater. Rounding yet another bend in the tunnel you are following, you are startled to discover you are not alone down here, but not as surprised as the woman who has been left gagged and bound hand and foot, resting with her back against the rocky wall.

It is a redheaded woman dressed in a practical but slightly masculine linen shirt, tweed waistcoat and plus fours. Her hair looks like it had been dressed neatly on top of her head, no doubt to keep it out of her eyes, but stray tresses have started to come loose and now dangle about her alabaster pale face, putting you in mind of the waving arms of a sea star. As does the pendant she is wearing on a silver chain around her neck.

Your eyes meet hers, but you do not see fear there, only a burning anger.

"Dr Addison, I presume?" you say, dropping to your knees and starting to undo the knots keeping her bound. Her hands free, you move on to untying the rope around her ankles.

"Who are you?" she demands, pulling the cloth gag from her mouth.

You introduce yourself, explaining that it was you she had been corresponding with via telegram regarding her search for the lost pirate ship.

"I went to the hotel, but when you didn't show up for our meeting as arranged, I started to look for you," you conclude.

"Well, thank goodness you did," says Dr Addison.

"But what happened to you? How did you end up here, gagged and bound?"

"I'll explain later." Dr Addison seems dismissive of your concern for her. "Right now, we must get out of here. Come on!"

With that, she sets off along the tunnel, giving the impression that she knows where she's going.

Make a fate test. Roll one die, and if you have the Weakness **{CURSED}**, deduct 1.

If the result is equal to or lower than the current doom level, turn to **236**.
If the result is greater than the current doom level, turn to **12**.

137

You step away from the open treasure chest but cannot take your eyes off the gold piled within. It speaks to something deep inside your soul.

Make a resolve test. Roll one die, add your **WILLPOWER** and your **SANITY**. You may spend **1 RESOURCE** to roll two dice and pick the highest. If you have the **{MYSTIC}** or **{SORCERY}** Ability, add 1. If you have the **{CURSED}** or **{TROUBLED DREAMS}** Weakness, deduct 1. What's the result?

Total of 12 or more: turn to **178**.
11 or less: turn to **55**.

It will take a steady hand to steer the boat through the treacherous waters around Devil Reef and so you choose to stay at your post, while exhorting Dr Addison to grab a boat hook and use it to drive off the creatures that are boarding your vessel in ever-increasing numbers.

But Dr Addison is an academic, not a fighter, and soon falls foul of the boarding party. As she flails at one of the fish-men with the hooked pole, the creature seizes her improvised weapon with one powerful hand and pulls it from her grasp. In the next moment, another of the creatures makes it to the gunwale and pounces on her, like some hideous humanoid toad.

You watch all of this through the spray-drenched windows of the wheelhouse, unable to do anything to help the wretched woman.

But her ultimate fate remains a mystery to you as more of the fish-people board your boat. They force their way into the wheelhouse and you do your best to defend yourself, but it is already too late.

You and Dr Addison will share a watery grave at the bottom of the Atlantic Ocean, while your boat will finally come to rest on the rugged rocks of the Innsmouth shore, destined to join the list of other unaccounted for wrecks along this stretch of the New England coast.

Take the Secret: *Davy Jones's Locker.*

The End.

Keeping to the shadows, of which there are plenty, you negotiate the corridors of the canning plant, using the piles of packed crates that seem to be everywhere for cover whenever you see someone coming your way.

Some doors open onto storage cupboards while others admit you to untidy rooms or yet more passageways. You look for a dropped handkerchief, an esoteric sigil smeared in grease on a filthy surface, anything that might indicate whether the academic visited this place before you. You don't want to ask any of the factory's employees for fear of drawing attention to yourself.

Eventually, you climb a steel staircase to a landing that looks down over the cannery's main production line. A series of conveyor belts wind their way around the barn-like space, tended by a phalanx of mindless human drones. At one end, a conveyor carries fish and other less identifiable things dredged up from the seabed to where workers armed with butcher-sharp cleavers and gutting knives fillet them after removing their heads, fins, and tails. They are then cooked and deposited into tins. At the other end of the line, the canned goods are transferred into boxes, ready to be distributed all over New England.

Spend either 1 clue or 1 resource or take +**1 DOOM**.

Almost hypnotized by the process, you watch for several minutes, choked by the potent smell of fish guts and brine. But it is then that a woman working on the factory floor happens to catch sight of you. She pauses, reaching for another cardboard box to pack with cans. Then, pointing, she alerts her supervisor, a bald man with bulging eyes and almost no chin at all.

There is only one thing for it: you are going to have to flee this place.

Roll one die and deduct 1 if you have the {**AGILE**} Ability.

If the total is equal to or less than your **HEALTH**, turn to **159**.
If the total is greater than your **HEALTH**, turn to **169**.

140

You successfully find your way to the cobbled Town Square. A branch of the First National Grocery chain stands on the square, while a signpost points the way to the Gilman House Hotel. You agreed to meet Dr Addison at the hotel at 2:00PM but you are two hours early.

How do you want to spend the time between now and 2:00PM?

Visit the First National Grocery: turn to **160**.
Explore the town: turn to **128**.
Make your way to the hotel and wait for Dr Addison there: turn to **83**.

141

Closing your eyes, despite the very real threat to life that is hanging over you now, you start to chant under your breath. The words of the mantra help you focus your thoughts, and you imagine building the great stone walls of a fortress around your mind, shielding it from the horrifying fish that has risen from the depths to claim the prize you now hold in your white-knuckled grip.

Turn to **291**.

142

In reality, the "book" is a cheaply produced pamphlet containing the predicted tide times for the week and printed locally. You find today's date and scan the list of times for today's tides. You notice that the time for low tide – 16:36 – has been circled in pencil, while in the margin, in a neat hand, has been written, "Accessed from beach?" However, you find nothing else jotted down inside the pamphlet. Take **+1 CLUE** and the **[BOOK OF TIDE TIMES]**.

A sudden noise outside the room makes you start. It sounded like something being dragged along the hallway outside. You freeze, barely daring to breathe, as the shuffling footsteps move away along the corridor.

What do you want to do now?

Continue to examine the papers on the table: turn to **111**.
Leave the hotel without delay and go in search of Dr Addison: turn to **101**.

143

With no magazines or copies of the local newspaper to help pass the time, there is nothing to do but watch the peeling yellow wallpaper while you wait. Pareidolia is soon in full effect and has you seeing patterns in the patches of damp and the minuscule tears in the paper.

At first these images take the form of trees and clouds and even fish. But then you imagine you can see movement within the patterns, like writhing tentacles, lapping waves, and indescribable things moving beneath them. And all the time the elderly front desk attendant watches you without ever saying a word. Does he know something you don't?

Take -**1 SANITY**, the Weakness **{PARANOID}**, and the SECRET: *The Yellow Wallpaper.*

With your sense of unease increasing with every passing minute, in the end you decide there is nothing to do but make your way to Dr Addsion's room and see if she is there.

Turn to **233**.

You are unable to tear your gaze from the monstrous figure. It is not because you are repulsed and therefore morbidly fascinated by it; it is because you feel you share some measure of kinship with it.

You walk the length of the hall toward the statue, not one of the gathered faithful raising a hand to stop you, and only come to a halt when you reach the foot of the dais.

Staring into the fish-god's polished, pearl-like eyes, you see a warped reflection of yourself. But it is not the familiar face you are used to seeing, but something new. Something rich and strange.

It is the new you that you see reflected there, the you that will join your new brothers and sisters one day in the deep trenches beyond Devil Reef, where you will swim and play within the hallowed halls of Y'ha-nthlei with the other children of Father Dagon and Mother Hydra.

The End.

You have barely entered the submerged tunnel when you are overwhelmed by a rising sense of panic, convinced that if you swim any farther, you will be condemning yourself to a watery grave. You imagine your final breath escaping your lungs, brackish water rushing to fill the vacuum.

Arms and legs flailing in fear, you turn back and kick your way to the surface, spluttering and gasping for air.

Take -1 **WILLPOWER** and the SECRET: *Panic Attack*.

You now have no other choice but to try to retrace your route through the subterranean labyrinth.

Turn to **15**.

146

You start asking around among the fishermen and wherrymen who have their boats moored along the southern edge of the harbor. They are reluctant to engage you in conversation, but when they learn that you want to head out to Devil Reef, they immediately turn away or tell you to be on your way.

"What do we do now?" Dr Addison asks, the frustration clear in her voice.

But you do not have an answer for her.

"I'll take you," comes a gruff voice from behind you. It belongs to a burly lobsterman who refused to help you five minutes ago.

"Thank you," you say. "What made you change your mind?"

He grunts. "You can pay?"

"Yes, I have money," Dr Addison replies.

"Then step this way," the lobsterman says, leading the way back down the quay to where his trawler sits rocking on the water. At the foot of the boarding plank, he waits for you and the academic to go first. "Please, after you."

But it is only as he boards the ship behind you that you feel the hairs rise on the back of your neck. Something's wrong.

Before you can voice your concerns, something hard hits you on the back of the head and you fall to the deck, unconsciousness. Take -**1 HEALTH**.

Take the SECRET: *Red Herring One.*

Roll one die and deduct 1 if you have the {**SURVIVOR**} or {**TOUGH**} Ability.

If the total is equal to or less than your **HEALTH**, turn to **298**.
If the total is greater than your **HEALTH**, turn to **13**.

"Can I help you?" you ask the men pointedly. Surprised by your boldness they slow their steps to a halt.

"I think the question should be: can we help you?" says the largest of the brutes. His voice has an unpleasant gargling quality, as if his throat is thick with phlegm.

"You could tell me the best way to get to the Town Square from here."

Make a **WILLPOWER** test. Roll one die and add your **WILLPOWER**. Alternatively, you may spend **1 RESOURCE** to roll two dice instead, pick the highest, and then add your **WILLPOWER**. If you have the {**SORCERY**}, {**POLICE**}, or {**DETECTIVE**} Ability, add 1. What's the result?

Total of 10 or more: turn to **68**.
9 or less: turn to **127**.

148

"Is that right?" the police officer replies dismissively.

"Yes," you reply, fixing him with a steely stare. You bite back the anger his reaction has provoked in you. "That is right, Deputy Constable Ropes. A woman's life could be at stake here, so I suggest you start taking this matter seriously."

Make a credibility test. Roll two dice and add both your **INTELLECT** and your **WILLPOWER**. If you have the {**CIVIC**} Ability, add 1. What's the total?

12 or more: turn to **168**.
11 or less: turn to **273**.

Using the metal key that comes with the tin to wind back the lid, you inhale the oily, fishy aroma of the sardines before popping a few into your mouth. They taste just as you would expect and, not realizing how hungry you were, you empty the rest of the tin's contents into your mouth.

It is only after you have finished your impromptu snack that you remember the stories of the curious-looking fish that are hauled up from the depths of the sea off Innsmouth. You can only hope there really were sardines in the can and not something… else. Take +**1 HEALTH** but +**1 DOOM** as well.

Exiting the small storage room, you set about looking for signs that Dr Addison might have visited the cannery too.

Turn to **139**.

You start to make your way down the beach, which brings you closer to the monsters, and you keep the powerful talisman still held high above your head. "I insist! The statue will keep them at bay."

Dr Addison gives a huff of annoyance but doesn't dare let you out of her sight.

"And where do you propose we go?" she asks as the two of you run the length of the jetty.

"Around the coast to Rockport, or maybe north to Newburyport," you reply. "But definitely not back to Innsmouth."

"Agreed," she says.

Reaching your boat, the two of you climb on board and, having handed the [GREENSTONE STATUE] to Dr Addison for safekeeping – which she accepts with greedy delight – you untie the hawser and cast off. The engine starts the first time. Taking the wheel, you steer the vessel away from Falcon Point.

Dr Addison continues to watch the goings-on at the beach from the security of the wheelhouse. Billows of fog roll in over the sea, obscuring the presence of the seaborne colossus. But then the clouds clear for a moment and there is no sign of the leviathan. It would appear that the fish-god has sunk beneath the waves again.

It is then that you feel the boat lurch.

Dr Addison turns to face you, panic in her eyes. "What was that?"

Before you can reply, a crash reverberates through the hull, throwing you hard against the wheel and sending Dr Addison reeling. Could you have hit a submerged reef? But you didn't think there were any shoals along this stretch of coast.

As you open your mouth to speak, the world turns around you. You are flung about the cabin as the boat overturns and the hold begins to flood.

Something enormous has risen from the sea, right beneath the ship, capsizing it in the process. But that is of little concern to you now. The [GREENSTONE STATUE] is gone, dropped by Dr Addison as the ship was upended and is even now sinking toward the bottom of the ocean. The academic is lying on top of the cracked windshield, blood blooming in the water that is pooling around her forehead, as the cabin fills with water.

Grabbing her, you fight the flow of water and swim out of the wheelhouse, dragging the unconscious academic with you as your boat continues to sink. Now, if you can only make it to land…

But the spawn of Dagon has other plans for you. Scaly hands seize hold of you from below and pull, dragging you under the foaming waves. Other hands take hold of Dr Addison and pull her under the water as well.

As the surface recedes into darkness above you, the pressure in your lungs building as you fight to hold your breath, you look down.

The creatures that have a hold of you, and are dragging you into the abyssal depths, are fish-like figures. But beyond them, far away through the gloom, you fancy you can see the glow of bioluminescence outlining colossal structures that look like sunken palaces, towers, and temples buried beneath – or perhaps even formed from – ancient accretions of coral.

And then you can hold your breath no longer.

You can only hope that, thanks to your sacrifice, the [GREENSTONE STATUE] is now lost to the fish-people at the bottom of the deep, deep ocean.

Take the SECRET: *The Supreme Sacrifice.*

Final score: 2 stars.

The End.

"I think you were right all along," you tell Dr Addison. "I believe the pirate queen's treasure is hidden in the tunnels under the town."

"I knew it!" she exclaims, vindicated. "And I think I know precisely where! We have to get back there immediately."

"It's going to be risky," you point out. "We'll be heading back to their lair. Into the shark's mouth, as it were."

"I know, that's why we mustn't delay."

Dr Addison bundles her research notes into a leather satchel and the two of you hurry down the stairs and out of the Gilman House Hotel.

You knew that heading back to the tidal tunnels would be dangerous, but you hadn't realized just how dangerous. You haven't even made it back to the shoreline when you become aware of the fact that you are being followed.

Half a dozen rough-looking men are pursuing you along the rundown street you are currently traversing, although a glance over your shoulder makes you wonder if "men" is quite the right word to describe them.

Fearing for your life, you pick up the pace only to see another four like them emerge from shadowed doorways ahead of you, trapping you in an ever-tightening net of ne'er-do-wells.

Two thugs seize Dr Addison while other callused hands go to grab you. But you are not going to be taken so easily... or so you think, until something hard connects with the back of your skull and you lose consciousness instantly.

Take -**2** **HEALTH** and the SECRET: *Red Herring Two*.

Roll one die and deduct 1 if you have the {**SURVIVOR**} or {**TOUGH**} Ability.

> If the total is equal to or less than your **HEALTH**, turn to **298**.
> If the total is greater than your **HEALTH**, turn to **13**.

152

Following the tracks left in the sand, your way illuminated by the radiant fungal growths, it does not feel like you have gone very far before you find yourself in a drier cave that is clearly being used to store crates, but crates of what? The bioluminescence is just as bright, however, and you can see that someone has left a [**CROWBAR**] leaning against one of the boxes. You use it to pry off the lid of one of the wooden boxes. Inside are glass bottles that can only contain one thing – moonshine!

> If you want to open a bottle and sample its contents, turn to **216**.
> If you want to see if any other tools have been left lying around in addition to the [**CROWBAR**], turn to **196**.
> If you would rather be on your way in the hope that Dr Addison could be somewhere nearby, turn to **136**.

"I like your attitude," Dr Addison says. "Or is it your greed for gold? Either way, we are going to find the lost treasure of Mèng Yáo."

"What have you discovered about the treasure's potential resting place?" you ask the treasure hunter.

Dr Addison starts to lay out the clues she has found regarding the resting place of the pirate queen's strongbox. There are three significant pieces of information. The first is the copy of a map that was tattooed onto the body of a former pirate, who was purported to have sailed with Mèng Yáo and somehow survived, showing this stretch of New England coast. The second is a transcription of the same man's deathbed confession; despite being only semi-coherent at the time, as he was dying from dengue fever, he kept talking about the treasure being hidden in a system of caves.

But the strangest piece of evidence is a sea shanty that is supposed to have originated in the region and which the academic has written out in full:

Full sail the ship had crossed the seas,
And the name of the ship was the Golden Breeze.
Long time it sought a harbor's ease.
Come listen to our song!
Soon will the seas arise
And lightning split the stormy skies.
Lord Dagon, hear our cry,
And take us all below!
On reaching these New England sands,
No peace was found on sea or land.
Poor ship it went down with all hands,
O listen to our song!

Soon will the seas arise
And lightning split the stormy skies.
Lord Dagon, hear our cry,
And take us all below!
Into the waves the captain fell,
No wish had she to drown in Hell.
To shore she came, and all was well.
Come join us in our song!
Soon will the seas arise
And lightning split the stormy skies.
Lord Dagon, hear our cry,
And take us all below!
And washed ashore her treasure chest – she
Vowed to hide it 'neath the nest – and
Ever since it's laid at rest,
So, sing we all our song!
Soon will the seas arise
And lightning split the stormy skies.
Lord Dagon, hear our cry,
We'll live with you below!

It is possible you may have also uncovered some information that might help you track down Mèng Yáo's lost loot.

If you think you know where it is hidden, turn to **276**.
If not, but you have both the [TREASURE HUNTER'S CHART] and a [LOGBOOK], turn to **182**.
If you have just one of these items, turn to **166**.
If you do not have either of these things and have no idea where the treasure is buried, turn to **17**.

154

Reaching the foot of the lighthouse, you climb the steps to the door in its base, which you can see is ajar. Take the SECRET: *The Lighthouse.*

"Hello?" you say habitually as you put a hand to the wood.

The door is pulled open sharply from the other side and a figure flies out of the tower. The man is holding an oil lantern in one hand, and it is by this light that you take in the horror that is the lighthouse keeper.

Beneath a sou'wester and framed by a tangle of gray curls, thanks to some severe dermatological condition, horrific injury or ungodly mutation, he appears to be as much a fish as he is a man. His skin has the appearance of malformed scales, while his eyes are like two pearls, each devoid of either pupil or iris. His blunt nose is receding into his face, while his black-lipped mouth is a gaping maw crammed with irregular, needle-like teeth.

In his other hand, he is holding a rusty boat hook, but the fingers wrapped around it are connected by webs of translucent skin and his fingernails are more like sharpened claws.

It is hard to read the man's emotions on his malformed face. Is he angry that you have been so bold as to trespass on his property, or is he simply surprised to find you standing at the threshold of his home?

He gives an unintelligible, sibilant hiss and thrusts the boat hook at you, forcing you backward off the top step.

How will you react?

Aggressively, ready to fight: turn to **202**.
Placatingly, hoping to diffuse the situation: turn to **192**.

Your heart is already beating fast, but it quickens still further as the bone-chilling water takes your breath away. Taking a moment to adjust and then filling your lungs as best you can, you dive down and swim toward the eerie blue glow.

You are right! It is a tunnel, but as its walls close in around you, you have no idea how far you will have to swim before you will be able to surface and breathe again.

Make a courage test. Roll one die and add your **WILLPOWER**. You may spend **1 RESOURCE** to roll two dice and pick the highest. If you have the Weakness {**CLAUSTROPHOBIA**}, deduct 2. What's the result?

Total of 8 or more: turn to **133**.
7 or less: turn to **145**.

156

"I think that very unlikely," the hotelier says, addressing you for the first time since you entered the guest house.

"But there was water coming under the door," you insist.

"Somebody probably spilt a glass of water by accident," comes the man's infuriatingly calm reply. "We take great care to ensure the plumbing is in excellent order."

If that's true, it's the only thing that is well maintained around here.

You begin to doubt your powers of persuasion. Take **-1 WILLPOWER.**

If you want to ask the man for the key to Room #428 instead, turn to **76**.

If you would rather wait in the hope that he will eventually have to leave the front desk, turn to **56**.

If you want to go back upstairs and try to break into Dr Addison's room, turn to **41**.

Dashing over to the window, you throw up the shades. Peering out, you are disappointed to see nothing in the way of a fire escape but only a long drop to the cobbled courtyard below. You freeze as a wave of dizziness causes your stomach to lurch. A crash, as of somebody throwing themselves at the hotel room door, snaps you out of your state of vertigo-induced paralysis.

Gain the Weakness **{FEAR OF HEIGHTS}**.

But you are committed to this course of action now. To both the left and right, ancient brick buildings butt up against the hotel. Their slanted roofs present a more reasonable distance to jump from your current position on the top floor. If you could use the windowsills on this side of the hotel as a ledge, albeit a very narrow one, you might be able to reach the abutting buildings and get down that way.

Easing yourself out of the window, you prepare to make your bold move.

Make a determination test. Roll one die and add your **WILLPOWER** and your **HEALTH**. If you have the **{AGILE}** Ability, add 1 to the result, or add 2 if you have the **{CLIMBER}** Ability. What is the total?

12 or more: turn to **197**.
11 or less: turn to **177**.

There are two things within reach which could prove useful – a steel [**HARPOON**] and the heaped mass of a fishing net – but which one do you want to grab to use against these malformed denizens of the deep?

To grab the [**HARPOON**], turn to **87**.
To use the fishing net, turn to **73**.

You race back down the stairs and, dodging any factory workers you encounter – who all seem to have the same staring, slack-jawed expression on their faces – you make it back to the entrance before anyone can stop you.

Emerging into the dull, overcast afternoon, you still wince at the change in light levels, so gloomy was it inside the canning plant. The goons on guard are slow to react to your sudden presence and you flee the factory. However, you do not stop running until you are several streets away, by which point you are panting with exhaustion.

Take **-1 HEALTH** and the Weakness **{WATCHED}**, and the Secret: *A Kettle of Fish*.

Turn to **28**.

The First National Grocery stands out from all the other establishments on the Town Square because it is the only one that is not in a ruinous state of repair. Inside, you find a well-stocked store with all manner of fresh and preserved foods on offer. A couple of Innsmouth residents slowly trudge the aisles at the back of the store. At the entrance, the young man standing behind the till clears his throat loudly. When you instinctively turn to see who made the noise, he catches your eye.

The youth is wearing a smartly pressed white shirt, the sleeves rolled up to the elbows, a clean white apron, and a bow tie. "Good day," he says with a cheeriness that is a counterpoint to the anxious expression on his face. "What brings you to Innsmouth this fine day?"

Peering out of the door at the overcast sky, you wouldn't consider the day particularly fine, but you do feel compelled to respond.

If you want to tell him the truth, turn to **215**.
If you want to make something up, turn to **180**.

As you turn the metal over in your hands, its lustrous surface shows your reflection, but warps it as would the looking glasses in a funhouse hall of mirrors. Your eyes appear to bulge unnaturally, while your jowls sag and, turning your head left and right, you believe you can see deep creases in the wrinkled skin of your neck.

Deduct **2 RESOURCES** and record the [**SEA GOLD**] on your Character Sheet, but also take **+1 DOOM**.

Having pocketed the [**SEA GOLD**], what do you want to do now?

> Take a closer look at the carved idols, if you haven't done so already: turn to **47**.
> Survey one of the more unusual items on offer: turn to **67**.
> Leave Henderson's Oddities: turn to **84**.

Standing before the living god of the spawn of Innsmouth, you feel as if the entity's mere presence threatens to shatter your mind.

You were wrong. The malign intelligence you sensed did not come from the [**GREENSTONE STATUE**]. That intelligence belonged to the monster before you and the sensation was a precursor to the coming of the one from the deep. You can feel it now, probing the defenses of your subconscious, as if seeking to subdue you with a mere thought.

You tighten your grip on the idol, believing now that if you were to let it go, you would be torn limb from limb by the foul beings in an instant. It is clearly important to the monsters.

If you have the {**SECRET RITES**} Ability, turn to **141**.
If not, turn to **113**.

Staring at the statue of the fish-monster, you find it equally appalling and appealing. What is happening to you?

Make a resistance test. Roll one die and add your **WILLPOWER**. If you have the {**SORCERY**} Ability add 2 to the result. What is the total?

9 or more: turn to **144**.
8 or less: turn to **134**.

The aging hotel manager is still standing there at the reception desk and gives you a sidelong glance as you stride past him without stopping and out the front door.

It is the middle of the afternoon and the sky overhead is the color of mackerel skin. Fed up with waiting for Dr Addison to turn up at the hotel, you decide to go in search of her.

You consider the places you know of around town. You wonder if any of them could be where the academic is at, or if any of them might be able to provide you with information as to her current whereabouts. Maybe she visited one of the local businesses unique to the fishing port, which might be of interest to an academic such as her, places like the curio shop called Henderson's Oddities or The Little Bookshop.

Then again, she has come to this moldering, half-drowned town in search of a shipwreck. Perhaps she is reconnoitering the shoreline, or maybe she has gone down to the harbor to see if she can hire a boat to take the two of you out into the bay and lost track of time.

As you consider the harbor and the unique businesses hereabouts, the Innsmouth Cannery rises like a leviathan on the horizon. It dominates the skyline beyond the harbor, looking like some monstrous sea beast beached amidst the derelict warehouses of the factory district. Surely it has nothing to do with Dr Addison's search for the wreck of the pirate ship, but perhaps it has had the same hypnotic effect on her as it appears to be having on you.

So where do you want to go in search of the errant academic?

Henderson's Oddities: turn to **45**.
The Little Bookshop: turn to **91**.
Down to the shore: turn to **126**.
Innsmouth Harbor: turn to **82**.
The Cannery: turn to **281**.

165

"I think the treasure is hidden in the town jail," you tell Dr Addison.

"Really?"

"Or under it."

"There are rumors that some of the tidal tunnels connect to passages under Innsmouth Jail," the academic says.

That as good as confirms it to your mind, and it doesn't take long for Dr Addison to come around to your way of thinking. She bundles her research notes into a leather satchel and the two of you hurry down the stairs and leave the Gilman House Hotel.

You're not far from the jail when you get the feeling that you are being followed. Looking back over your shoulder, you see that half a dozen rough-looking types are trailing after you.

Fearing for your life, you pick up the pace only to see another four men emerge from shadowed doorways ahead of you, trapping you in an ever-tightening net of ne'er-do-wells.

A pair of thugs seizes Dr Addison while other callused hands grab you. But you are not going to be taken so easily... or so you think, until something hard connects with the back of your skull and you lose consciousness.

Take -2 **HEALTH** and the SECRET: *Red Herring Three*.

Roll one die and deduct 1 if you have the **{SURVIVOR}** or **{TOUGH}** Ability.

> If the total is equal to or less than your **HEALTH**, turn to **298**.
> If the total is greater than your **HEALTH**, turn to **13**.

166

You consider first where the pirate queen's junk is likely to have gone down and then the closest land Mèng Yáo could have reached and, therefore, where she is likely to have hidden her ill-gotten booty.

Make a deduction test. Roll one die and add your **INTELLECT**. Alternatively, you can spend **1 CLUE** to roll two dice instead, add them together, and then add the sum to your **INTELLECT**. And if you have any of the following Abilities – **{DETECTIVE}**, **{SAILOR}**, **{SEEKER}**, **{STUDIOUS}** – add 1 to the total.

What is the final result?

10 or higher: turn to **125**.
9 or less: turn to **17**.

167

Turning tail, you set off at a run back the way you came, not caring in which direction you are headed, only that it is away from these Innsmouth troublemakers.

Roll one die and deduct 1 if you have the **{TOUGH}** or **{SURVIVOR}** Ability.

If the total is equal to or less than your **HEALTH**, turn to **36**.
If the total is greater than your **HEALTH**, turn to **48**.

"Very well," says the officer. He takes a blank form from a drawer and you see the words "Missing Person Report" printed at the top. "So, who is it that's gone missing?"

"Dr Stella Addison of Miskatonic University."

Deputy Constable Ropes starts to fill in the form as you provide him with as much information as you can, such as the presumed time of her disappearance and where Dr Addison was last seen.

When you visited the academic's room at the Gilman House Hotel, you may have acquired one or more of the following items: [BOOK OF TIDE TIMES],[DR ADDISON'S DIARY],[INNSMOUTH TRIBUNE].

Which do you have?

[BOOK OF TIDE TIMES] only: turn to **3**.
[DR ADDISON'S DIARY] only: turn to **23**.
[INNSMOUTH TRIBUNE] only: turn to **43**.
[BOOK OF TIDE TIMES] and [DR ADDISON'S DIARY]: turn to **103**.
[BOOK OF TIDE TIMES] and [INNSMOUTH TRIBUNE]: turn to **123**.
[DR ADDISON'S DIARY] and [INNSMOUTH TRIBUNE]: turn to **183**.
None of them: turn to **213**.

169

You race down the stairs only to find a gaggle of angry workers waiting for you at the bottom. You don't know why they are so unhappy to find you inside the cannery but, no matter the reason, you are going to have to fight your way past them if you hope to escape the factory. You can't allow yourself to be cowed by the presence of so many blubbery faces, either.

You may spend **1 RESOURCE** at the start of each round to add 2 to your total for that round.

Round one: roll two dice and add your **COMBAT** and your **WILLPOWER**. If you have the **{ROGUE}** Ability, add 1. If the total is 14 or more, you win the first round.

Round two: roll two dice and add your **COMBAT** and your **WILLPOWER**. If you have the **{SURVIVOR}** Ability, add 1. If you won the first round, add 2. If your total is 15 or more, you win the second round.

If you won both rounds, turn to **199**.
If you lost one or more rounds, turn to **189**.

As you make your way around town, you feel eyes on you everywhere you go.

If you have the Weakness {**WATCHED**}, turn to **7**.
If not, turn to **34**.

You ask if Dr Stella Addison has visited Henderson's Oddities.

"I don't think so," the proprietor replies. "We don't get many outsiders visiting Innsmouth and I'm usually pretty good with faces. What does she look like?"

Having never met her yourself, you cannot help him in that regard.

"It's been very quiet of late in the shop," Jack confesses. "Is she here studying the tremors?"

"The tremors?"

"Yes, you know, the seaquakes, or whatever it is they call them. They've been recorded out near Devil Reef and Falcon Point, I believe."

"No, her particular area of interest is the recovery of antiquities," you explain.

"You must tell me more. Let me make us some coffee. I think I've got an open packet of cookies somewhere as well." He disappears through an archway behind the counter. His voice continues to carry from whatever back room he has moved to. "Feel free to have a browse while the coffee's brewing."

Still having no idea where Dr Addison has got to, you don't feel you can spend much more time here shooting the breeze over a pot of java. But the oddities from which the shop gets its name exert a strange pull. Take -1 **WILLPOWER**.

If you want to examine the esoteric artifacts, turn to **37**.
If not, turn to **201**.

"On my way up to see my friend, I couldn't help noticing water coming under the door of Room #212 on the second floor," you tell the elderly gentleman. "Maybe somebody left a tap running or a pipe has sprung a leak."

The hotel manager regards you with that same impassive stare as you elaborate on your fabrication, but does he believe you?

Make a persuasion test. Roll one die and add your **WILLPOWER**. Alternatively, you may spend **1 RESOURCE** to roll two dice instead, add them together, and then add the sum to your **WILLPOWER**. If you have the **{SORCERY}** Ability, add 1. What's the result?

Total of 8 or more: turn to **96**.
7 or less: turn to **156**.

173

As you approach the room to the right – Dr Addison hissing at you to hurry – the hypnotic, chanting voices draw you ever onward until you pass through the doorway and enter what, to your mind at least, can only be described as a temple.

The walls are adorned with magnificent murals and mosaics, depicting wondrous aquatic vistas – magnificent cities and palaces set amid kelp forests, and home to all manner of fish and other deep-dwelling creatures, everything from sharks and gigantic manta rays to crabs and squid, as well as other less recognizable things.

But the most unreal and extraordinary portrayals are of the eerily humanoid creatures shown swimming with the shoals of fish at the bottom of the sea.

On the far side of the chamber, two tall windows frame a raised dais, on top of which is a huge statue of a kneeling figure holding a great platter above its head. The effigy would be twice as tall as a man if it stood erect, and it depicts something that is both man and fish at the same time, like the figures in the murals. It has long, muscular limbs, while a tall fin protrudes from the top of its head and runs down its back, and its wide mouth is full of shark-like teeth.

You barely notice the cultists who have gathered within this place on this particular night to worship the ones who dwell in the deep. There are other three-dimensional representations of such fish-human hybrids within the room shown wielding tridents and standing atop columns of what you take to be coral. But you are transfixed by the statue on the dais.

As you stare into the pearl-like eyes of the effigy, the gurgling voices of the faithful swell.

What is the current doom level?

5 or more: turn to **144**.
3-4 or less: turn to **163**.
2 or less: turn to **134**.

Leaving Devil Reef far behind, you are not troubled by any more of the warped denizens of the deep as you continue toward Falcon Point, your little boat powering through the mountainous gray waves.

Eventually, through the fog, the shining beacon at the top of the lighthouse appears to rise above you, and then you are abruptly presented with a great wall of black rock rising out of the sea. You have reached the promontory.

A poorly maintained jetty projects from the shore, which is composed of sea-worn stones. Still, it's better than being forced to weigh anchor out in the bay and then swim the rest of the way or having to plough the prow of the boat into the beach, such as it is.

Grabbing a lit [OIL LANTERN] from the wheelhouse, you leap down from the gunwale to the jetty. Tying the boat off – you don't want it drifting off to be consumed by the fog – you help Dr Addison from the boat and onto the uneven planks.

The two of you take a moment to examine the cliff face before you. Somewhere beneath that vast outcrop of black rock lies the lost treasure of Mèng Yáo the pirate queen.

Turn to **220**.

175

In the semi-darkness, with no sun above or obvious landmarks to guide you, after an hour of wandering the tidal tunnels, you are totally lost. Not only do you not have any idea where Dr Addison might be, you are not sure you will ever be able to find your way out again. But try you must.

And so, you press on until the twisting passageway you are following brings you to a dark pool and presents you with a dead end. Or is it? You can see the same bioluminescent glow coming from within the pool, suggesting that the tunnel might continue, but underwater.

At the risk of getting both wet and cold, you could enter the pool and see if your supposition is correct. But if you don't want to do that you are going to have to do your best to retrace your steps.

So, what's it to be?

To enter the pool, turn to **155**.
To attempt to retrace your steps, turn to **15**.

176

"Oh good," Chief Constable Martin says, his voice a guttural growl. "I like it when they won't go quietly."

The two policemen both come for you then, batons in hand. You have no choice but to defend yourself as best you can against the beating they intend to dish out. You may spend **1 RESOURCE** at the start of each round to add 2 to your total for that round.

Round one: roll two dice and add your **COMBAT**. If you have the **{TOUGH}** Ability, add 1. If the total is 13 or more, you win the first round.

Round two: roll two dice and add your **COMBAT**. If you have the **{FIGHTER}** Ability, add 1. If you won the first round, add 2. If your total is 14 or more, you win the second round.

Round three: roll two dice and add your **COMBAT**. If you have the **{SURVIVOR}** Ability, add 1. If you won the second round, add 2. If your total is 15 or more, you win the third round.

If you won the third round, turn to **89**.
If you lost the third round, turn to **49**.

With your arms and legs shaking in response to the adrenaline racing through your bloodstream, you pull yourself upright on the windowsill outside the room. Shuffling your toes along the ledge, you reach the void between this window and that of the next room along. It is a good four feet between the edge of the sill you are balanced on and the leading edge of the next.

The rapid beating of your heart pounding in your ears, you steel yourself to make the jump. But just as you are about to launch yourself across the void, the door to Room #428 crashes open, making you jump.

Startled, you lose your footing and with nothing to grab onto other than the rough brickwork above the window, you topple off your precarious perch.

You hit the cobbles below with bone-crunching force, breaking your neck in the process. Death is instantaneous.

The End.

Closing the lid of the chest, you retrace your steps through the cave until you are standing at the top of the rock slope and loose earth left by the landslide.

You are greeted by the billows of fog that blanket the sea and the susurrus of the surf sucking at the stones of the beach. It sounds like an old man with few remaining teeth slurping the last dregs of fish soup from a bowl.

Taking care not to trigger a secondary landslip, you set off back across the shoreline. But you come to a skidding halt when you catch sight of the welcoming committee that is there to greet you.

Through the vaporous murk, you can see row after row of figures rising from the sea and stepping out of the surf onto the beach. Every single one of them is humanoid to a greater or lesser extent, and they all walk on their hind legs, but some of them look like they would be more at home under the sea than on the land. A leaner figure leading the march is wearing a sea-soaked coat and a tricorn hat.

"If the treasure is ever found, Mèng Yáo will return from the sea to claim it herself," Dr Addison says in a faraway voice, as if repeating something she has been told.

You instinctively know what the new arrivals want. But what can you do against so many? There must be at least two dozen here, with more still rising from the ocean's depths behind them.

To charge down the beach and engage the tricorn-wearer in battle, turn to **240**.
To try something else, turn to **256**.

179

Dr Addison shoves her research notes into a leather satchel and the two of you leave the Gilman House Hotel.

You're not far from The Little Bookshop when you get the feeling that you are being followed. Looking back over your shoulder you see that you are indeed being followed by half a dozen rough-looking thugs.

Fearing for your life, you pick up the pace only for another four men to emerge from shadowed alleyways ahead of you, ensuring you are trapped within an ever-tightening ring of ruffians.

Two of the thugs seize Dr Addison, while two more go for you. But you decide you are not going to be taken so easily… that is until something hard hits you on the back of the head and you fall to the ground, having lost consciousness.

Take -**2 HEALTH** and the SECRET: *Red Herring Four*.

Roll one die and deduct 1 if you have the **{SURVIVOR}** or **{TOUGH}** Ability.

> If the total is equal to or less than your **HEALTH**, turn to **298**.
> If the total is greater than your **HEALTH**, turn to **13**.

180

The name badge pinned to the anxious-looking young man's shirt pocket reads: Brian Burnham, Manager. You tell Brian that you are a curious sightseer visiting all the most famous locations along this stretch of coast, from Newburyport to Salem.

Make a persuasion test. Roll one die and add your **WILLPOWER**. Alternatively, you may spend **1 RESOURCE** to roll two dice instead, add them together, and then add the sum to your **WILLPOWER**. If you have the Weakness {**CRIMINAL**}, deduct 1. What's the result?

Total of 8 or more: turn to **191**.
7 or less: turn to **204**.

181

"What else do you think you can tell me about the ship?"

"Can you tell me anything else about it?" Henderson asks, answering your question with a question. "Many ships have floundered on the reefs going back much further than seventy years."

Unfortunately, because you have not managed to meet with Dr Addison yet, you cannot tell him any more, and you get the impression the academic hasn't paid him a visit either.

"Hang on. Seventy years..."

"Or thereabouts," you say.

The young man's eyes suddenly light up. "That could mean it went down in the 1850s, which would tie in with the legend of the pirate queen of the Orient."

"The pirate queen of the Orient?" you echo in disbelief. "Here, off the coast of North America?"

"Yes." Jack nods excitedly.

Running a finger along the shelf of logbooks, he stops and pulls a slim volume from between its fellows. It looks less like a journal and more like a sheaf of papers held together in a leather portfolio. Placing it on a convenient table, he opens it and rifles through the papers within. They are covered in handwritten notes. While you cannot make head nor tail of them from where you stand, Henderson clearly knows what he's looking for.

"Yes, here it is. Her name was Mèng Yáo, meaning 'beautiful vision,' but she was far more ruthless than her name might suggest. Legend has it that her junk, the Golden Breeze, sank off Falcon Point during a terrible storm."

He passes you the **[LOGBOOK]**.

"And I suppose legend also has it that the Golden Breeze was carrying a fortune in treasure at the time," you say.

"Not quite. Supposedly Mèng Yáo managed to make it to land and buried at least some of her ill-gotten booty."

"And where was that?" you ask.

"As with all the best pirate legends, nobody knows," Henderson says with a wry smile. "Perhaps you'll be the one to find it."

"But what happened to the pirate queen?" you ask.

"According to this particular account, she was killed by her bosun, who also survived the shipwreck, when she wouldn't tell him where she had hidden her gold. But I've come across another version of the tale that says she killed her crew herself, so that none of them could reveal where she had hidden her treasure. As she was leaving the cave where she had supposedly buried her strongbox, there was a landslide that buried the entrance. In the process, she slipped and fell into the sea and was never seen again."

"Of course."

"But there is another myth that persists that if her treasure is ever found, Mèng Yáo will return from the sea to claim it."

"Similar to many good sea dog's tales," you put in with a grin.

Take +**1 CLUE** and the SECRET: *Dead Men Tell No Tales.*

What do you want to do now?

Ask Jack if he has encountered Dr Addison: turn to **171**.

Take a look at some of the stranger items for sale in the shop: turn to **37**.

Leave Henderson's Oddities: turn to **201**.

Taking out the [**TREASURE HUNTER'S CHART**] you spread it on the table so both you and the doctor can study it. Recalling your conversation with the proprietor of Henderson's Oddities, you consider what the legends say about where the pirate queen hid her treasure in light of the physical evidence.

Make a deduction test. Roll one die and add your **INTELLECT**. You can spend **1 CLUE** to roll two dice and pick the highest. And if you have any of the following Abilities – {**DETECTIVE**}, {**SAILOR**}, {**SEEKER**}, {**STUDIOUS**} – add 1 to the total.

What is the final result?

> 8 or higher: turn to **125**.
> 7 or less: turn to **17**.

"I was supposed to meet Dr Addison at the Gilman House Hotel," you explain to the duty constable, "but she never showed. I managed to gain entry to her room" – at this Deputy Constable Ropes raises a suspicious eyebrow – "and I found a copy of the *Innsmouth Tribune* among her things. It was folded open on an article about seismic activity that has been recorded in the area and another concerning the new cannery."

"Ah yes," says Ropes, "another venture undertaken by the beneficent Marsh family. Old Man Marsh and his family have done a lot for this town; more than you'll ever know. If your friend really has gone missing, you can be sure it has nothing to do with the Innsmouth Cannery or the Marsh family. Did you find anything else in her room that might have given you an idea where she could have gone?"

"Her diary. But the only thing written in there that might be relevant were the names of two locations: 'Tidal Tunnels' and 'The Little Bookshop.'"

"And have you tried looking for this Dr Addison at either of those places?" Deputy Constable Ropes puts down his pen and looks at you pointedly. You don't like how his tone has changed either. Take **+1 CLUE** and the Weakness **{WATCHED}**.

Turn to **213**.

184

You feel slightly uncomfortable reading the doctor's diary, as if you are invading her privacy by doing so. But needs must...

Finding today's date, you see "2:00PM" written in pencil and your initials next to it. There are no other appointments recorded in the diary for this week. However, scribbled across the bottom of the page is the following note:

Tidal Tunnels under town – entrance exposed at low tide.
Link to The Little Bookshop?

Having already crossed a line by reading [DR ADDISON'S DIARY], you decide to cross another one and take the diary with you.

What would you like to do next?

Take a closer look at the [BOOK OF TIDE TIMES]: turn to **142**.
Examine the [INNSMOUTH TRIBUNE]: turn to **132**.
Leave the room, and the hotel, and go in search of Dr Addison: turn to **164**.

185

The ones who have crept from the deep to thwart your plans may have been cowed by the power emanating from the grotesque effigy of the fish-god, but something else lives below the waves, directing the tides as well as its spawn, that will not succumb so readily to the power of the Atlantean artifact.

The surface of the dark ocean beyond Falcon Point heaves

then and something gargantuan breaks the surface. It surges forth from the boiling waves like the legendary leviathan spoken of in the book of Job.

Black water cascades from the immense scaled form as it rises from the sea, with no sign that it is going to stop. The ocean spray and persistent fog leave the giant as an oppressive shadowy being that appears nonetheless world-ending for all that. Take -1 **SANITY** and the SECRET: *Deep Rising.*

In the presence of the colossal creature, the statue grows hot within your grasp and the waves of dark power emanating from it throb as if in time with a booming heartbeat.

Has this god made flesh risen from the freezing depths of the ocean in answer to the effigy's call? Or is it here to reclaim the treasure itself?

And if the artifact can hold sway over an army of the fish-people, could it have a similar effect on this monstrous entity?

Otherwise powerless, when faced by the might of the leviathan, the only thing you have in your possession that you can imagine would have any hope of protecting you from the creature is the **[GREENSTONE STATUE]**.

But how best to use it against the monster?

If you want to hurl the effigy at the creature, turn to **50**.
If you would rather stay as you are, with the idol held high above your head, turn to **162**.

Wondering whose footsteps you are following – could they belong to Dr Addison? – you push forward into the cavernous network of tidal tunnels. Soon, however, the sand beneath your feet peters out, giving way to treacherous, uneven rock.

It isn't long before the passageway branches again. Investigating one branch, taking care to watch where you tread, you haven't gone far when it splits once again. With no idea of where the academic is, you do your best to navigate the labyrinthine tunnels.

Make a navigation test. Roll one die and add your **INTELLECT**. Alternatively, you can spend **1 RESOURCE** to roll two dice instead, pick the highest, and then add your **INTELLECT**. If you have the **{SEEKER}** Ability, the **[MAP OF THE TUNNELS]**, or the **[SHIP'S COMPASS]**, add 1 to the total. But if you have the **{CURSED}**, **{TAINTED LINEAGE}** or **{TROUBLED DREAMS}** Weakness, deduct 2 from the total.

What's the result?

Total of 11 or more: turn to **20**.
10 or less: turn to **175**.

Rounding the corner of a crumbling brick building, you find your way blocked by the same men whose sudden interest in you set you on this unwise path.

These Shoreward Slums lie largely empty, as the tenants of the degraded dwellings are no doubt employed at the Marsh Refinery or on board the numerous fishing smacks that dredge the waters beyond Devil Reef during the day. But they are never entirely empty, and it is plain that you have strayed into a place where outsiders are not welcome.

There are three of them, clad in flat caps, thick woolen jumpers, heavy trousers and hobnailed boots. The body language of the thugs suggests that they do not intend to let you off with a warning and one of them is casually carrying a broken plank over one shoulder.

What do you want to do?

Attempt to flee: turn to **167**.
Challenge the thugs: turn to **147**.
Prepare to defend yourself as best you can: turn to **127**.

188

Desperate times call for desperate measures. And perhaps some esoteric artifact will save you from these unfathomable hybrids of man and fish.

Which of the following do you want to use against the fish-people?

> [**SEA GOLD**], if you have some: turn to **29**.
> A[**CARVED IDOL**], if you have one: turn to **39**.
> If you do not have either of these items, turn to **51**.

189

There are simply too many of them and you are overcome by sheer force of numbers. You fall beneath their bludgeoning fists, although you do your best to mitigate the damage by curling up into a ball and wrapping your arms around your head.

Take -**2 HEALTH** and -**1 COMBAT**.

Roll one die and deduct 1 if you have the {**SURVIVOR**} or {**TOUGH**} Ability.

> If the total is equal to or less than your current **HEALTH**, turn to **298**.
> If the total is greater than your current **HEALTH**, turn to **13**.

190

Desperation gives you an advantage over the hired thugs – who are only in this for the money and the grim pleasure of beating you up – and the rush of adrenaline lends you the speed and agility to avoid knife thrusts and clumsily swung fists.

Dancing around the dockhands, you manage to get one of them to stab the other. As they start trading blows with each other in their anger, you see an opportunity and take it.

However, before you flee back along Sawbone Alley, you may pick up the [**FLICK KNIFE**] one of them has dropped. If you do so, take **+1 RESOURCE** and **+1 COMBAT**.

You get the feeling that if you are being hunted because you have been making enquiries about the whereabouts of Dr Addison, then she could be in trouble, too. You need to find her before it's too late!

Turn to **34**.

"Well, if I were you, I wouldn't stop here for long," he says, a haunted look in his eyes. "Joe Sargent's Bus Service will be along again this evening. Make sure you're on it when it leaves. I hear there are some very reasonable, and yet still comfortable, guest houses in Arkham. And there's far more to see there than here."

"Duly noted," you reply. "But as there's some time between now and then, what are the highlights I really shouldn't miss while I'm here in Innsmouth?"

The youth studies you uncertainly. Then, repurposing a piece of the paper he would normally use to wrap someone's sausages and taking a pencil from behind his ear, he starts to draw you a map of the town.

"You could head out along the breakwater," he says as he deftly draws the harbor in aerial view. "You'll get a good view of Devil Reef from there, sea and fog willing, but the Innsmouth Lighthouse at the end fell into ruin years ago. Heading into town, there are a few shops you might like to visit. Sightseers will find plenty to wonder at in Henderson's Oddities, and The Little Bookshop is worth a visit too." He marks these places on the map for you. "But whatever you do, steer clear of the cannery" – he circles a spot close to where the Manuxet River pours into Innsmouth Bay – "and certainly don't enter the slums that surround the Marsh Refinery." He points out another place on the map with his pencil before putting a large X through it. "They don't like strangers visiting that part of town."

You wonder who "they" are but decide not to press the young man as you fold up the map and secret it about your person. Take +**2 CLUES**.

"Before you go, is there anything else you would like?" he asks. "Something you might like to buy?"

If you would like to buy something, turn to **270**.
If you would rather leave and make your way to the Gilman House Hotel for your meeting with Dr Addison, turn to **83**.

You do your best to talk the lighthouse keeper down – telling him that you meant no harm and only came to investigate the lighthouse – but the more you try to placate him, the angrier he becomes.

"Your kind are not welcome here," he croaks, his pearlescent gaze locked on Dr Addison. And with that, he attacks.

You may spend **1 RESOURCE** at the start of each round to add 2 to your total for that round.

Round one: roll two dice and add your **COMBAT**. If you have the {**TOUGH**} Ability, add 1. If the total is 15 or more, you win the first round.

Round two: roll two dice and add your **COMBAT**. If you have the {**FIGHTER**} Ability, add 1. If you won the first round, add 2. If your total is 16 or more, you win the second round.

If you won the second round, turn to **227**.
If you lost the second round, turn to **214**.

193

At the end of the corridor, you turn a corner and descend the staircase that awaits you there, with Dr Addison still at your side. At the bottom, you find yourselves in a grand pillared hall. As you start to cross it, you realize that the two of you are being watched by the impassive faces of the great and good of Innsmouth, who stare down at you from the walls with frozen, watercolor and oil-painted eyes. Some of the paintings look like they date back to Innsmouth's founding and its heyday as a center for both fishing and shipbuilding.

Four pillars support the roof, but they are made from some dark stone that you have not seen used anywhere else in the construction of this place. Between the pillars stand several marble busts – of jowly, pompous-looking old men – and a few glass cabinets containing golden chains of office and opulent robes.

Overwhelmed by the extravagance of it all, you slow your steps. It is then that you become aware of the slapping footsteps – as of someone trying to run wearing frogman flippers – on the stairs behind you.

Turning, you see a gaggle of strangely garbed figures descending the stone staircase, their veiny, pallid arms outstretched toward you. They appear to be clad in little more than diaphanous robes of sapphire and emerald hue. You can only assume that these people are members of the Esoteric Order of Dagon and, as such, had a hand in your abduction and imprisonment!

How do you want to respond to their arrival?

To turn and make your last stand against the Order here, turn to **116**.
To take something from your pack to use against your pursuers, turn to **93**.
To send some of the exhibits crashing to the ground in your wake, as you flee the hall, turn to **284**.

You check the date and see that the paper is two days old. It has been folded so that your eye is drawn to the article at the bottom of the page, which bears the headline "Tremors Shake Innsmouth."

Apparently, there has been some recent seismic disturbance that has caused minor damage to property and the town's infrastructure, opening potholes in the coastal road and the like. The epicenter of this activity is thought to be off the coast, however, in the vicinity of Devil Reef, although there have also been reports of tremors as far away as Falcon Point.

A smaller piece on the same page is about the Innsmouth

Cannery. According to the article, it hasn't been open long, but the town's fortunes are already looking up because of the money the business is bringing into the town, thanks to the goods it produces being sold all over New England. Considering the derelict state of the town, is this honest journalism or merely a propaganda piece? Take +**1 CLUE** and record the [**INNSMOUTH TRIBUNE**] on your Character Sheet.

What do you want to do now?

> Examine the [**BOOK OF TIDE TIMES**]: turn to **142**.
> Open [**DR ADDISON'S DIARY**]: turn to **121**.
> Leave the room, and the hotel, and go in search of Dr Addison: turn to **164**.

"You think the treasure is hidden in the harbor?" Dr Addison says, sounding slightly bewildered when you tell her. "I suppose it could be in the tunnels under the lighthouse." And so, the two of you leave the hotel and head for the harbor.

Upon reaching the quayside, you are rather surprised to find a group of fishermen gathered there. If you didn't know better, you would think they were waiting for you.

As you set off along the breakwater they follow, and before long you realize you have walked into a trap. Nothing awaits you at the end of the causeway other than the ruined lighthouse and the sea. There is nowhere for you to go.

The fishermen soon catch up with you. Two of them seize Dr Addison and two go for you. But you are not going to be taken so easily… that is until a heavy cudgel – usually used for stunning fish – hits you on the back of the head and you fall to the ground, unconscious.

Take -**2 HEALTH** and the SECRET: *Red Herring Five.*

Roll one die and deduct 1 if you have the **{SURVIVOR}** or **{TOUGH}** Ability.

> If the total is equal to or less than your **HEALTH**, turn to **298**.
> If the total is greater than your **HEALTH**, turn to **13**.

196

As well as the **[CROWBAR]**, there is also a **[HAMMER]**.

Record any items you want to take on your Character Sheet. For each one you claim you may also take +**1 RESOURCE**.

When you are done, choosing something you haven't tried already, what do you want to do next?

> Sample some of the moonshine: turn to **216**.
> Leave the storage cave and resume your search: turn to **136**.

Adrenaline racing through your system, you pull yourself upright on the windowsill outside the room. Shuffling your toes along the ledge, you reach the void between this window and that of the next room. It is a not insignificant gap – a good four feet between the edge of the sill you are currently balanced on and the next.

The rapid beat of your heart pounding in your ears, trying not to look down, you steel yourself to make the jump. Taking a deep breath, you launch yourself across the divide.

You manage to plant the tips of your toes on the next windowsill and grab hold of the brickwork above to stop yourself falling to the courtyard below.

You hear a crash come from the room you have just left and surmise that whoever was outside the door has successfully forced their way in. This knowledge spurs you on to maintain your current course of action.

Edging along to the opposite end of the ledge, you do the same again until you are perched above the slanted roof of the abutting building.

Taking your life in your hands, you jump, landing on the angled tiles and sliding to the pipework of a rain gutter before you can stop yourself. However, compared to what you have accomplished already, it is a straightforward matter to make it down to ground level without excessive risk to life or limb.

You hear angry shouts from above and see two of the locals looking out a window, gesturing at you in obvious annoyance. You don't hang around but head out into the streets of Innsmouth instead.

There is nothing you can do for Dr Addison at present, so you hurry out of the courtyard and turn onto the street.

Moving at a trot, upon reaching the Town Square, you seek out its lonely bus stop – but Joe Sargent's Bus Service is not currently parked up there.

No matter, you will just have to leave town on foot. Bearing in mind that where you ran into trouble was north of the Manuxet River, your surest ways out of Innsmouth are either south along the coast road to Arkham, or by sea via the harbor.

Looking east, in the direction of the harbor, you are horrified to see a thick sea fog rolling in off the ocean. Dusk is already falling, but the advancing black-and-green-tinged fog is smothering everything within the fishing town in a cold, gray cloud. It is even suffocating the glowing streetlamps that are just coming on.

As the fog first blurs and then absorbs the surrounding buildings, thereby robbing you of any useful landmarks and stealing away your natural sense of direction, you become aware of other things moving within the murk. You spot one and then, soon after, a second and a third, and before long you come to the chilling realization that you are surrounded by shadowy figures.

The lumpen forms appear to be human, walking upright on two legs, but you strain to make out any more details. But it is the strange cries echoing through the fog that raises both your heart rate and the hackles on the back of your neck.

You can hear an amphibian croaking, an indefinable hooting, and unintelligible gibbering. And then there are the voices, although they sound like they are coming from throats clogged with phlegm and are not speaking in any language you understand.

You feel a creeping sense of dread and a cold knot of fear forms in the pit of your stomach. Then all your worst fears come to fruition as the figures close in and you see their hairless, slack-jawed faces and watery, wide-set eyes, and you know that you will never escape Innsmouth. You feel slimy hands seize you and a split second later something hits you across the back of the head and you lose consciousness. Take **-1 HEALTH**.

Roll one die and deduct 1 if you have the **{SURVIVOR}** or **{TOUGH}** Ability.

> If the total is equal to or less than your **HEALTH**, turn to **298**.
> If the total is greater than your **HEALTH**, turn to **13**.

198

"I think Mèng Yáo's treasure is buried somewhere along the Innsmouth shoreline," you tell Dr Addison.

"So, I was close with the tidal tunnels," she says, clearly feeling vindicated. "But if it's actually on the shore, I think I know the place – Smuggler's Drop! Come on, we must head back over there before sunset."

"It's going to be risky," you point out.

"I know, that's why we have to get there before dark."

Dr Addison bundles her research notes into a leather satchel and the two of you hurry down the stairs and out of the hotel.

You knew that heading back toward the coast would be dangerous, but you hadn't realized just how dangerous. You haven't even made it as far as the shoreline when you become aware of the fact that you are being followed.

Half a dozen rough-looking men are pursuing you along

the rundown street you are currently traversing, although a glance over your shoulder makes you wonder if "men" is quite the right word to describe them.

Fearing for your life, you pick up the pace only to see another four men emerge from shadowed doorways ahead of you, trapping you in an ever-tightening net of ne'er-do-wells.

Two thugs seize Dr Addison while other callused hands go to grab you. But you are not going to be taken so easily… or so you think, until something hard connects with the back of your skull and you lose consciousness instantly.

Take -**2 HEALTH** and the SECRET: *Red Herring Six.*

Roll one die and deduct 1 if you have the **{SURVIVOR}** or **{TOUGH}** Ability.

If the total is equal to or less than your **HEALTH**, turn to **298**.
If the total is greater than your **HEALTH**, turn to **13**.

199

Fighting your way past the men and women you encounter – who all seem to have the same staring, slack-jawed expression on their faces – against all odds, you manage to make it to the entrance of the factory.

Emerging into the dull, overcast afternoon, you still wince at the change in light levels, so gloomy was it inside the canning plant. The goons on guard are slow to react to your sudden presence and you flee the factory. However, you do not stop running until you are several streets away, by which point you are panting with exhaustion.

Take -1 **HEALTH** and the Weakness **{WATCHED}**, and the SECRET: *Slippery as an Eel.*

Turn to **28**.

By the smothered glow of the streetlamps, you can see the silhouettes of church spires looming up through the vapor around you. You seem to have lost anyone who might have been pursuing you.

"This is New Church Green," Dr Addison says breathlessly as you catch up with her. "That means the Manuxet River is south of here, and beyond that, the Town Square."

You might not be able to tell which way is north and which is south thanks to the ever-present fog, but Dr Addison seems to know and so you are happy to let her take the lead as she moves with purpose in a direction that you presume is toward the river. As long as you are heading away from the headquarters of the Esoteric Order of Dagon, you don't really care where you're going.

Reaching the bridge that crosses the meager stream that empties into the Innsmouth Harbor, you realize something is wrong. Through the fog, you can see webbed hands reaching over the bridge parapet as a dozen or more half-human horrors finish their climb from the lower falls below to the span of the bridge. On the other side lies the Town Square and a possible way out of Innsmouth. To remain here, you are sure, would mean certain death, so there really is no choice to be made.

You and Dr Addison both sprint toward the bridge and start to cross it as the fish-things pull themselves up onto the low stone wall, ready to spring. Your heart racing, you keep running, your legs burning with the effort, but you manage to evade the grasping claws of the creatures.

It is only when you are on the other side that you realize Dr Addison is no longer with you. Spinning round, you see her struggling against a knot of the amphibious fish-folk. But before you can do anything to help her, the creatures holding her dive back over the side of the bridge, taking the academic with them. You hear a splash far below and before the same fate can befall you, you race the last hundred yards to the Town Square.

Unbelievably, Joe Sargent's Bus Service is pulled up there. The rumble of its engine increases as it prepares to depart. But when it does leave, it is with you on board.

Peering through the window, you can see shadowy figures standing motionless within the perfidious fog. Why didn't they pursue you once you had crossed the bridge? Was it only Dr Addison they wanted all along?

As the bus swings round and turns onto Federal Street, you catch your reflection in the glass and see the same slack expression worn by so many of the residents of Innsmouth staring back at you…

Take the SECRET: *The Shadow Over Innsmouth.*

Final score: 3 stars.

Turn to **300**.

201

You make for the door, but you cannot take your eyes off the weird carvings and sea-worn pieces that look like they could be pieces of flotsam and jetsam collected from the shoreline by an entrepreneurial beachcomber.

Make a temptation test. Roll one die and add your **WILLPOWER**. You may spend **1 RESOURCE** to roll two dice and pick the highest. If you have any of the following Abilities or Weaknesses, deduct 1 from the total: **{ARCANE STUDIES}**, **{CURSED}**, **{HAUNTED}**, **{MYSTIC}**, **{SORCERY}**, **{TROUBLED DREAMS}**.

What's the result?

Total of 7 or more: turn to **84**.
6 or less: turn to **37**.

202

Convinced that the deformed creature can only mean you harm, you take the attitude that the best form of defense is attack and bring everything you have to bear against the lighthouse keeper. You may spend **1 RESOURCE** at the start of each round to add 2 to your total for that round.

Round one: roll two dice and add your **COMBAT**. If you have the **{FIGHTER}** Ability, add 1. If the total is 13 or more, you win the first round.

Round two: roll two dice and add your **COMBAT**. If you have the {**FIGHTER**} Ability, add 1. If you won the first round, add 2. If your total is 14 or more, you win the second round.

If you won the second round, turn to **227**.
If you lost the second round, turn to **214**.

203

The tide having withdrawn, it is now possible to access the largest of the openings that lie along this stretch of rocky shoreline. A narrow ledge, exposed by the receding waves, runs parallel to the cave wall, leading into the depths of the sea cave itself.

If Dr Addison has truly braved the tidal tunnels beneath Innsmouth, then surely this would have been the way she went.

Watching your step on the slippery rocks and always keeping one hand on the rising curve of the cave wall, you make it to the far end of the grotto. As your eyes adjust to the gloom, you see that the rock ledge gives way to a rising bank of sand; the mouth of a narrow tunnel, even darker than your current surroundings, provides you with the means to continue.

You can taste the salty tang of the sea air in the back of your throat, while your nose is picking up wafts of the ammonia smell of rotting crustaceans. All manner of detritus has been washed into the cave then deposited on the sandbank. Picking your way through the litter of kelp and the splintered shells of crabs the size of your head, you enter the tunnel.

As you reach the limit of the pale gray daylight's reach, you are surprised to find the way ahead suffused with a blue glow. Intrigued, you continue along a fissure that forms a natural passageway through the rock and soon discover the source of the bioluminescence. It is produced by not one but several different types of fungi that you have never come across anywhere else. They must be indigenous to this stretch of the New England coast.

Not much farther on, the tunnel splits. By the eerie glow, you can see indentations in the sand that could be footsteps heading off along the channel to the left, while the grooves of drag marks cover the floor of the spur to the right.

Take **+2 DOOM**. You may spend **1 CLUE** or **1 RESOURCE** to reduce the **DOOM** penalty by 1; spend **2 CLUES** or **2 RESOURCES** to avoid adding any doom.

Which branch do you want to follow?

To go right, turn to **152**.
To go left, turn to **186**.

204

"I'm sorry, but no one comes to Innsmouth on holiday," the young man says, his face darkening. "It's far too dangerous a place for tourists."

Take -**1 INTELLECT**.

Turn to **237**.

205

In a moment of cold realization, you find yourself wondering why are you resisting the sea-dwellers at all. They mean you no harm. They only wish to welcome you into their family of fish-folk and have you live with them under the sea. Life will be so much better when you join your new kin beneath the waves.

Lowering the arm holding the idol, you start to walk to where the waves are breaking on the beach as the creatures gathered there reach forth their arms to draw you to them.

"What's happening to you?" Dr Addison exclaims. "What's happening to your skin?" Her voice sounds to you as if it is coming from far away and you can barely hear what she is saying. Absentmindedly, you glance down at your hands, but you barely react to the sight of the scales forming on the exposed skin. You have become aware that your heart is beating in time with the steady ebb and flow of the tide.

The academic rushes forward and tries to claw the effigy from your hand. "What are you doing?" she screams, but you violently bat her away and she falls to the stones, winded and gasping for breath.

As you step forward and accept the cold embrace of the sea, you are only dimly aware of the doctor's muffled screams and a sound like someone sucking the meat from a turkey leg. But these noises trouble you not, now that your heart is filled with a new purpose: to join Father Dagon in the fathomless depths of Y'ha-nthlei.

Take the Secret: *Swimming with the Fishes.*

The End.

"What makes you think the treasure is there?" Dr Addison challenges you.

"I don't think it was buried there, but I think that its proprietor might know something of its whereabouts," you tell her.

Dr Addison throws her research notes into a leather satchel and the two of you leave the hotel. But you haven't gone far when you get the feeling that you are being followed. Looking back over your shoulder you see that half a dozen rough-looking thugs are trailing after you.

Fearing for your safety, you pick up the pace only for another four men to emerge from shadowed alleyways ahead of you, ensuring you are trapped within an ever-tightening ring of ruffians.

Two of the thugs seize Dr Addison, while two more go for you. But you decide you are not going to be taken so easily...

that is until something hard hits you on the back of the head and you fall to the ground, unconscious.

Take -**2 HEALTH** and the SECRET: *Red Herring Seven*.

Roll one die and deduct 1 if you have the **{SURVIVOR}** or **{TOUGH}** Ability.

> If the total is equal to or less than your **HEALTH**, turn to **298**.
> If the total is greater than your **HEALTH**, turn to **13**.

207

"I am trying to report the disappearance of a potentially vulnerable woman!" you rail. "I am not here to trick anyone or to spy on any association. I merely want to know what has happened to Dr Stella Addison!"

While you are in the grip of your own tirade, the duty policeman is joined by another, older officer, who emerges from a back room.

"Problem, Deputy Constable Ropes?" he asks laconically.

"Not at all, Chief Constable Martin," Ropes replies. "Just another troublemaker wasting police time."

"A night in the cells should put a stop to that sort of behavior."

"I agree, chief constable." At that, Ropes rounds the end of the counter and moves toward you. "You are under arrest for wasting police time."

This is preposterous, but what do you intend to do about it?

If you want to go quietly in the hope of sorting this out later, turn to **79**.
If you want to resist arrest, turn to **176**.

208

Realizing that the priest might not be the last member of the Esoteric Order of Dagon you encounter before you can escape this place completely, you grab him by his robes and haul him back to his feet, shoving him in front of you with one arm twisted up behind his back to stop him from getting away.

Leaving the robing room, you see several figures clustered at the opposite end of the corridor, seemingly being verbally threatened by Dr Addison to stay away. Her face is full of determined fear. The figures all have the same fish-eyed features as the priest and are just as lacking in hair.

He says something in a gargling, guttural tongue that you do not understand, but the cultists clearly do. They hang back as Dr Addison leads the way toward the end of the corridor.

Descending a curving stone staircase you come to a grand hall decorated with all manner of unnerving exhibits that only serve to heighten your desire to flee this place.

The relief you feel upon finally exiting the building is palpable. Releasing your hostage, you shove him to the ground and throw yourself down the steps outside the former Masonic Hall. But you are not out of danger yet.

You can hear the bare feet of the members of the Esoteric Order slapping on the stones of the steps as they chase after you and Dr Addison, who didn't wait around and is already far ahead of you.

Turn to **200**.

The sheer quantity of books on display in the shop is overwhelming and you continue to scan their spines, your curiosity piqued even as your frustration with the bookshop owner's organizational system, or lack of one, increases.

Make a pursuit of knowledge test. Roll one die and add your **INTELLECT**. You can spend **1 CLUE** to roll two dice and pick the highest.

What is the result?

8 or higher: turn to **62**.
5-7: turn to **71**.
4 or less: turn to **219**.

210

Descending into the darkness beneath Falcon Point, you step down onto sand and follow the winding path it takes between more great outcroppings of rock until you finally reach a dead end. As far as you can tell, the cave does not connect with the sea.

The sand here is smooth, having clearly lain undisturbed for many years. Chiseled into the wall is what you recognize to be a Chinese image shape, a kind of ancient pictogram, although you have no idea what it represents.

"Mèng Yáo's treasure chest is here," Dr Addison says in a barely suppressed whisper, pointing at the logograph. "It must be buried."

It looks like you are going to have to get digging.

If you are carrying a [**SPADE**], turn to **222**.
If not, turn to **232**.

211

As you swim across the pool, your attention fully focused on the way out, you imagine you can feel the cold orbs of the effigies' pearl-like eyes upon you, as if they recognize in you something like them. At the same time, a part of you echoes the silent call of the unearthly pantheon.

What is going on? Are you going mad? Take -1 **SANITY**.

If you have the {**TROUBLED DREAMS**} Weakness, turn to **221**.
If you have the {**ARCANE STUDIES**} Ability, turn to **231**.
If you have the {**ANCIENT LANGUAGES**} Ability, turn to **242**.
If you have none of these Weaknesses or Abilities, turn to **252**.

As you descend the worm-eaten stairs, with their dusty, frayed carpet, you formulate a plan that will enable you to acquire the key to Room #428.

It is common practice for guests to hand in their keys when they leave the hotel for the day but, even if Dr Addison is still in possession of her room key, the hotel will no doubt keep a spare. You could simply ask the hotel manager to lend you the key, pointing out that you are a professional acquaintance of the academic and there on request. Or you could wait, hoping that the man will have to leave the front desk at some point, at which time you could lift the key. Alternatively, you could try to trick him into leaving his post and borrow the key when he's not looking.

Returning to the hotel lobby, which approach do you want to employ?

Ask the hotelier for the key to Room #428: turn to **76**.
Wait for the man to leave his position: turn to **56**.
Try to trick the man into leaving his post: turn to **172**.

"Leave it with me," Deputy Constable Ropes says, having finished filling out the missing persons form, "and I'll let you know if there are any developments. Where can you be contacted while you are in town?"

"The Gilman House Hotel," you reply without really thinking.

You get the feeling that Officer Ropes will file the form in the round filing cabinet in the corner as soon as you have left the building, but other than continuing to search for Dr Addison yourself, you're not sure what else is to be done.

If you want to leave the Innsmouth Jail, turn to **253**.
If you want to push the officer regarding what his next course of action will be, turn to **273**.

The lighthouse keeper is relentless and for fear of succumbing to his blows altogether, you turn and run. Take -1 **HEALTH** and +1 **DOOM**.

"Come on! This way!" Dr Addison shouts. She is already some way ahead of you, making for the edge of Falcon Point. You only hope that the deranged lighthouse keeper doesn't choose to pursue you, having already succeeded in driving you off.

You soon find yourself standing right at the edge of the precipice, the cliff face curving away beneath you in a vertiginous drop. However, it is not a sheer cliff and there is a precarious way down, lacking anything that would arrest your fall should you slip, such as a handrail, or even a few iron rungs hammered into the rock.

"There's nothing else for it," Dr Addison says, also considering the dizzying descent. "If we're going to recover Mèng Yáo's booty, we are going to have to tackle that perilous path."

So you set off, but with Dr Addison leading the way down. It takes a great deal of concentration as you consider each step cautiously before committing to it.

Make a concentration test. Roll one die and add your **INTELLECT** and your **WILLPOWER**. Alternatively, you may spend **1 RESOURCE** to roll two dice instead, add them together, and then add the sum to your **INTELLECT**. If you have the Weakness **{FEAR OF HEIGHTS}**, deduct 2. If you have the **{AGILE}** Ability, add 1. And if you have the **{CLIMBER}** Ability, add 1. What's the result?

Total of 11 or more: turn to **255**.
10 or less: turn to **244**.

215

You tell the shopkeeper how you have come to Innsmouth in response to an advert placed in the *Arkham Advertiser* by one Dr Stella Addison, to aid her in the search for a pirate ship that sank hereabouts some seventy years ago.

He stares at you in horror as you reveal your reason for being in town and when you've finished speaking, he says, "You must leave immediately. Do not go to that meeting. Get on the next bus out of town and do not look back!" He keeps his voice low so that the other people in the shop cannot hear.

You are so shocked by the vehemence of the young man's reaction that you consider doing just as he says.

If you want to leave the store immediately, turn to **226**.
If you demand to be told what he is talking about first, turn to **237**.

You uncork one of the glass bottles and the potent fumes of the alcohol hit you immediately, making you recoil as your eyes start to water. But you've come this far, so you put the bottle to your lips and take a swig.

It feels like the liquid is burning the inside of your mouth but, rather than spit it out, you instinctively swallow. The moonshine stings your throat, making you cough, before hitting your stomach, rapidly producing a sensation like heartburn in your chest.

However, despite feeling like you are drinking paint thinner, the burning soon subsides and is replaced with a warmth that spreads through your entire body. Not only that, but you feel your resolve strengthening: you are ready to take on anyone who might challenge you down here.

Take +1 **HEALTH**, +1 **COMBAT**, +1 **WILLPOWER**, and the SECRET: *Aqua Vitae*. However, also take +1 **DOOM**. You may take the bottle of [**MOONSHINE**] with you, if you like.

Choosing something you haven't done already, what do you want to do now?

See what other items have been left lying around: turn to **196**.
Leave the storage area and resume your search for Dr Addison: turn to **136**.

Without hesitation, you run at the door connecting Dr Addison's room to the one to the south and, twisting your body at the last moment, hit it with your shoulder. The wood around the lock and bolt holding the door shut splinters and you fly through it into the adjoining bedroom.

You are delighted to discover that this one is free of occupants – paying guests or otherwise – and make for the door that leads to the corridor, with Dr Addison hot on your heels. This door proves to be unlocked but, as you open it a crack and peer through to see if the coast is clear, you notice an [**UMBRELLA**] resting in a stand next to you.

If you want to take the [**UMBRELLA**] with you, take **+1 RESOURCE** and record it on your Character Sheet.

At that moment, you hear a crash as the intruders succeed in forcing their way in at last. At the same time, you and Dr Addison scamper out of Room #427 unnoticed by whoever is hunting you, your footfalls muffled by soft carpet.

Take **+1 INTELLECT** for your quick thinking.

Turn to **26**.

218

The repulsive priest is stronger and a more capable fighter than he looks, but you are overcome as much by his repulsive appearance as you are by his combat prowess. His blows take their toll on your body and you retreat from the robing chamber, employing what strength you have left to escape this accursed place. Take -**1 HEALTH.**

Turn to **268**.

219

It is no good; the arrangement of the titles is too chaotic, the motivations of the one who arranged them in such a way inscrutable.

You turn from the bookshelves, the names of myriad titles and authors still swirling before your eyes.

To speak to the shop's proprietor, turn to **229**.
Alternatively, you could simply leave the premises.
If you have had enough of this place, turn to **35**.

Scrambling across the beach, you discover evidence of a recent landslide. In fact, it looks like part of the cliff face has broken away, exposing the distinct edges of clean, unweathered rock beneath. More excitingly, this geological activity has revealed the gaping mouth of a cave entrance, although you are going to have to scale the scree left by the landslide to access it.

"This must be it!" Dr Addison declares. "After all, I do not see where else it could be hidden on this promontory."

You lead the way, with Dr Addison following the route you take almost step for step.

Reaching the top of the mound of rock and earth, you find yourself within the open maw of the cave. As you pass through it, you cannot shake the feeling that you are willingly entering the gullet of some colossal leviathan.

> If you are carrying an [**OIL LANTERN**], [**LIGHTER**], or [**FLASHLIGHT**], turn to **210**.
> If not, turn to **230**.

An image suddenly flashes into your mind; it is as if the two lesser statues have come to life and you see them – scaled, malformed monstrosities that they are – cavorting amid forests of kelp, deep beneath the sea. And they are not alone – their spawn is with them too, a multitude of pallid fish-men spinning and twisting in the deep ocean currents amidst pillars of rock that might be natural formations or might just as easily have been sculpted by clumsy, clawed hands.

What does this mean for the world above the waves? Spend either 1 clue or 1 resource or take **+1 DOOM**.

If you have the {**ARCANE STUDIES**} Ability, turn to **231**.
If you have the {**ANCIENT LANGUAGES**} Ability, turn to **242**.
If you have neither of these Abilities, turn to **252**.

Making good use of the [**SPADE**] you have risked life and limb to carry down here, before long you have dug several pits in the sand covering the cave floor and are rewarded at long last when the blade strikes something hard under the sand that isn't yet another rock.

Clearing more of the sand from the hole, you finally uncover an aged wooden chest, exposing it to the air for the first time in seventy years, or so Dr Addison's research would have you believe.

Take the SECRET: *Spadework*.

Turn to **243**.

223

If there is one element that epitomizes the derelict condition of the entire harbor, it is the abandoned rundown lighthouse that stands at the tip of the breakwater. You make your way slowly along the sea wall in the direction where the lighthouse stands far away, wondering what could have befallen it to cause such a ruinous state now.

Turn to **294**.

224

"It looks like we're going to be best off going by land," you tell the academic.

It's not far to Falcon Point as the crow flies, but because of the inlet-riddled coastline in this part of Massachusetts, it's still going to be a good hour's walk, so you set off straightaway. Besides, you don't want to give the locals time to work out where you're going.

As the fog rolls in off the sea, blanketing the land, you are robbed of any landmarks and lose all sense of direction. But

Dr Addison still seems to be able to tell where she is going, so you follow her lead.

Despite the fog and encroaching darkness, you make it to Falcon Point in under an hour and a half. As you approach the headland, a zephyr comes in off the sea, carrying with it the smell of salt and cold, and the banks of fog swirl and part momentarily, affording you a view of the promontory ahead.

Falcon Point rises from the ocean as a great wall of black rock, perpetually battered by the unforgiving waves. Atop the blasted headland, the sweeping beam of a lighthouse struggles to penetrate the mist that clings to the promontory with its damp, webbed fingers.

Making it to the gatehouse that marks the boundary between the land and Falcon Point, you push open the untended iron gates and begin to climb the trail that leads to the lighthouse.

Fifty yards ahead of you, the well-worn, stony path you are following splits. The branch to the left appears to lead straight toward the cliff and beyond that, the sea. The right-hand branch continues to climb the headland, at the top of which stands the lighthouse. However, not far from the foot of the beacon you can see the shadow of what you take to be the lighthouse keeper's cottage.

In which direction do you want to go?

Toward the cliff edge: turn to **234**.
Toward the lighthouse: turn to **296**.
Toward the lighthouse keeper's cottage: turn to **266**.

In reality, the "book" is a cheaply produced pamphlet containing the predicted tide times for the week and printed locally. You find today's date and scan the list of times for today's tides. You notice that the time for low tide – 16:36 – has been circled in pencil, while in the margin, in a neat hand, has been written, "Accessed from beach?" However, you find nothing else jotted down inside the pamphlet. Take **+1 CLUE** and the **[BOOK OF TIDE TIMES]**.

What do you want to do now?

> Examine the **[INNSMOUTH TRIBUNE]**: turn to **132**.
> Read **[DR ADDISON'S DIARY]**: turn to **121**.
> Leave the room, and the hotel, and go in search of Dr Addison: turn to **164**.

You hurry out of the First National Grocery and find yourself back in the cobbled, semi-circular Town Square. There is no sign of a bus or any other vehicle for that matter. Approaching the bus stop, you check the timetable and see that the bus won't stop here again until this evening.

You suddenly get the feeling that someone is watching

you. Goosebumps rise on your skin. You spin around but can see no one. What has gotten into you? Take -**1 SANITY** and -**1 WILLPOWER**.

You are jumping at imagined phantoms. Angry at yourself, as much as anyone, you march back into the grocery store, intending to ask the young man precisely what he is playing at, scaring away potential customers like that.

Turn to **237**.

227

The lighthouse keeper is tough, and his heavy raincoat protects him from some of your blows, but in the end, you prove to be more than a match for the man, if you can even call him that.

Gibbering in fear, he runs back inside the lighthouse but drops the [**OIL LANTERN**] he was carrying. If you want to take this item, record it on your Character Sheet and take +**1 RESOURCE**.

"If you're quite done?" Dr Addison chastises, having done

nothing to help in your fight with the lighthouse keeper. "This way!" With that she sets off toward the edge of the cliff with a purposeful stride.

If you want to follow Dr Addison, turn to **234**.
If you want to stop off at the lighthouse keeper's cottage first, if you haven't done so already, turn to **249**.
If you want to follow the man into the lighthouse, turn to **269**.

The priest is not a skilled fighter, but he is so repulsive you still recoil from making contact with him. He is not particularly strong either, although he is solidly built. You soon get the better of him.

Make an inspiration test. Roll one die and add your **INTELLECT**. You may spend **1 CLUE** to roll two dice and pick the highest. If you have the **{QUICK-WITTED}** Ability, add 1. What's the total?

8 or more: turn to **208**.
7 or less: turn to **268**.

"Good afternoon," you say, addressing the woman, who gives the impression that she is hiding behind the barricade of books piled on the table in front of her.

Lost in the tome she is reading, it takes her a moment to register that you are talking to her. "May I help you?" she asks, her tone edged with irritation now that her reading time has been interrupted.

You take in the framed postcards, knickknacks, and the other homely touches that help create such a welcoming atmosphere, even if the woman's manner doesn't.

"I like what you've done with the place."

"I take it you're just visiting our town," she says, her demeanor thawing. You nod. "Is there anything I could help you with? My name is Joyce, by the way. Joyce Little. Proprietor of The Little Bookshop."

If you have [DR ADDISON'S DIARY], turn to **257**.
If not, turn to **267**.

You pause at the entrance to the cave as the academic pushes past you and starts to descend into the cave.

"Come on!" she calls back. "What are you waiting for?"

> If you have the {**SORCERY**} Ability, turn to **210**.
> If not, turn to **241**.

During your studies of the esoteric and arcane, you have come across the gods of an antediluvian age in art, literature and even archaeological dig sites. Effigies such as these three would not have been placed in this dripping cave for no reason.

Indeed, the presence of the deities transforms this sea-carved cave into a sacred place, a place of reverence and worship. You are at the heart of a temple. But where are the worshippers? Take +**1 CLUE**.

> If you have the {**ANCIENT LANGUAGES**}
> Ability, turn to **242**.
> If not, turn to **252**.

232

Wishing you had a spade to make the task at least a little easier, you make do with what you have at hand and join Dr Addison in digging one pit after another in the sandy floor of the cave.

It is slow and tiring work, but you eventually uncover what looks like wood at the bottom of a shallow pit. Clearing more of the coarse sand away with your hands, you are delighted to find that the wood is the corner of an old chest. But this doesn't change the fact that you are exhausted.

Take -**1 HEALTH**, -**1 COMBAT**, and the SECRET: *Buried Treasure.*

Turn to **243**.

233

Approaching the reception desk, you ask the elderly hotelier which room Dr Stella Addison is staying in. He glances down at the ledger in front of him before replying that she is in Room #428 on the top floor. He does not challenge you as you walk toward the stairs and, upon reaching the top floor, you find the room you are looking for.

You knock on the door and wait. Hearing nothing from the other side, you knock again, calling out her name. "Dr Addison?"

You wait a little longer this time, but when there is still no response you try a third time. "Dr Addison, are you there?"

Apparently, she is not.

Perhaps the curious atmosphere that pervades the town is getting to you, but you start to imagine all sorts of dire ends for the academic. Are they truly ridiculous flights of fancy or has something actually happened to Dr Addison?

There is only one way you are going to find out and that is by entering her room. She could be lying unconscious within, in need of medical aid.

You try the handle and while it turns, the door remains shut. It is clearly locked.

How do you want to proceed?

Go back downstairs and get the room key: turn to **212**.

Try to force your way in: turn to **41**.

Being very careful where you put your feet, fully aware that if you were to trip and fall it could end in disaster, you head toward the edge of the cliff. After all, the treasure you seek is hidden in a cave under Falcon Point, or so you believe.

You soon find yourself standing right at the edge of the precipice, the cliff face curving away beneath you in a vertiginous drop. However, it is not a sheer cliff, and there is a perilous way down, lacking anything that would arrest your fall should you slip, such as a handrail, or even a few iron rungs hammered into the rock.

"There's nothing else for it," Dr Addison says, also considering the dizzying descent. "If we're going to recover Mèng Yáo's booty, we are going to have to tackle that path."

So you set off, but with Dr Addison leading the way down. It takes a great deal of concentration as you consider each step carefully before committing to it.

Make a concentration test. Roll one die and add your **INTELLECT** and your **WILLPOWER**. Alternatively, you may spend **1 RESOURCE** to roll two dice instead, add them together, and then add the sum to your **INTELLECT**. If you have the Weakness **{FEAR OF HEIGHTS}**, deduct 2. If you have the **{AGILE}** Ability, add 1. And if you have the **{CLIMBER}** Ability, add 1. What's the result?

Total of 10 or more: turn to **255**.
9 or less: turn to **244**.

Dr Addison's room is as dismal as the rest of the hotel. Two windows look out over a dingy courtyard hemmed in by low, deserted brick blocks. Through the grimy panes you can also see the unfarmable, waterlogged countryside that lies beyond the dilapidated roofs of the decaying town.

The décor of the room is dreary, the furnishings cheap and poorly made. There is no sink in the room, the occupant being expected to make use of the musty, communal bathroom at the end of the hall.

There is a bed, a rickety wardrobe, and a small table against one wall with a chair beside it. What there isn't, is any sign of Dr Addison, but the way everything has been left would imply that the occupant of the room fully intends to return. The academic clearly hasn't checked out. But she has still missed your appointment.

Your attention is drawn to the pile of papers that have been heaped haphazardly on the table. Rummaging through them you find three items of particular interest: a [**BOOK OF TIDE TIMES**]; a copy of the [**INNSMOUTH TRIBUNE**]; and what is quite clearly [**DR ADDISON'S DIARY**].

What do you want to do?

Flick through the [**BOOK OF TIDE TIMES**]: turn to **225**.
Take a closer look at the [**INNSMOUTH TRIBUNE**]: turn to **194**.
Open [**DR ADDISON'S DIARY**]: turn to **184**.
Leave the room, and the hotel, and go in search of Dr Addison elsewhere: turn to **164**.

236

Dr Addison leads the way back through the tunnels, brushing off any questions you have about her recent experiences. She is clearly not of a mind to talk about what has happened to her, which you find surprising.

Finally, you enter a cave which you can see leads to the sea. However, the only thing that tells you this is the tiny arc of half-light you can see on the opposite side of the chamber. The cave mouth has been almost completely submerged by the rising tide.

Dr Addison curses under her breath.

But the incoming tide is not the worst of it. As you watch the eddies swirling at the mouth of the cave, threatening to extinguish that sliver of daylight at any moment, a trio of domed heads breaks the surface.

They are gliding toward you and, as they draw nearer, you realize that they belong to three curious creatures that are even now emerging from the water. In the restricted light of the cave, you only see them as silhouettes, but they appear to be crudely human in form.

If you stay where you are, you are going to have to confront the creatures. But if you run back into the tunnels, who knows if you will ever get out of here?

"Come on, this way! We have to go back!" Dr Addison snaps, pulling on your arm.

If you want to do as Dr Addison says and run for it, turn to **10**.
If you would rather stand and face your fate, turn to **246**.

237

"My name is Brian, Brian Burnham, and I am the manager of this store," the young man says when you challenge him. You can hardly believe it – he barely looks old enough to shave! "I may not have been here long, but I've been here long enough to know that the fine folks of Innsmouth don't take kindly to visitors."

He glances in the direction of the other customers at the back of the shop before going on in a hushed whisper: "You do not want to still be in Innsmouth when night falls. It is certainly not wise to be out and about after dusk, either."

"What do you mean?" you ask.

"I mean people have gone missing – people not from Innsmouth – after dark."

If you want to press Brian Burnham for more information, turn to **248**.
If not, turn to **259**.

238

Instinct tells you that the [OCTOPUS CROWN] is precious to the priest, and so you snatch it from its resting place on the cushion.

He gives a gurgling cry that sets his jowls and the rolls of flesh around his neck quivering, and he goes to grab the artifact from you. In response, you hold the crown above your head with one hand whilst using the other to indicate that he should halt if he doesn't want any harm to befall the treasure.

With the priest caught in a quandary – desperately needing to reclaim the crown and yet, at the same time, not wanting anything untoward to happen to it – he remains where he is, whimpering in obvious distress as you back out of the room still holding the golden octopus.

Take +2 **DOOM**. You may spend **1 CLUE** or **1 RESOURCE** to reduce the **DOOM** penalty by 1; spend **2 CLUES** or **2 RESOURCES** to avoid adding any **DOOM**.

Where do you want to go now?

Through the other door: turn to **173**.
Head for the end of the corridor: turn to **193**.

239

"You're a visitor to Innsmouth?"

The enquiry makes you look up with a start. Standing not three feet from you is the bookshop's proprietor.

"Yes," you say, closing the book in haste, slightly flustered.

"That's an interesting choice," she says, eyeing the book's cover. "Is there anything I could help you with? My name is Joyce, by the way. Joyce Little. Proprietor of The Little Bookshop."

If you have [**DR ADDISON'S DIARY**], turn to **257**.
If not, turn to **267**.

240

Hoping that if their leader is defeated the others will disperse and return to Davy Jones's Locker – or Atlantis, wherever it is they came from – you issue a challenge and bound over to engage the creature in one-to-one combat. Dr Addison yells something and you hear her following behind.

As you draw closer, you see that your chosen target is no mysterious Chinese woman returned from a watery grave but a malformed monster, part human being and part fish. You cannot begin to guess what happened to the real Mèng Yáo, but this cannot be her.

But there's no changing your mind now. The creature is already upon you. You may spend **1 RESOURCE** at the start of each round to add 2 to your total for that round.

Round one: roll two dice and add your **COMBAT** and your **WILLPOWER** but then deduct the current **DOOM** level. If you have the Weakness **{CURSED}**, deduct 2. If you have the **{SURVIVOR}** Ability, add 1. If the total is 12 or more, you win the first round.

Round two: roll two dice and add your **COMBAT** and your **WILLPOWER**. If you have the **{TOUGH}** Ability, add 1. If you won the first round, add 2. If your total is 13 or more, you win the second round.

If you won the second round, turn to **260**.
If you lost the second round, turn to **6**.

It is too dark for you to see your way into the cave, and you dare not risk spraining an ankle when you consider what you could encounter upon returning to the wave-lashed shore.

"If you find anything down there, you can keep it!" you shout back, your words echoing within the cavernous space.

And so, you sit down and gaze out over the fogbound sea. The sound of the surf sucking at the stones of the beach is like a toothless old man slurping his soup. But then comes another sound – the crunch of footsteps on gravel.

Peering through the vaporous murk, you can make out row after row of figures rising from the sea. Every single one of them is humanoid in form, to a greater or lesser extent, and they all walk on their hind legs, but some of them look like they would be more at home underwater than on dry land.

You scramble to your feet, readying yourself for flight or fight. But in reality, it is too late for either.

The surface of the dark ocean beyond Falcon Point heaves and something gargantuan breaks the surface. It surges forth from the boiling waves like the legendary leviathan spoken of in the book of Job.

Big enough to kill a whale with its bare hands, you have no hope against the sea god as it reaches for you with one immense, clawed hand…

Take the SECRET: *Fish Supper.*

The End.

242

Each of the statues stands upon a carved stone plinth. Among the carvings are images of fish-people playing in stylized waves or paying homage to creatures very much like these monstrous deities. As well as the graven images, on the base of each of the smaller statues there is also a kind of cuneiform script that is not entirely unfamiliar to you.

You cannot help but attempt to decode what it says. The base upon which the bloated effigy sits bears a pictogram that means "nurturer" or "protector," followed by what would appear to be a name: "Hydra." The other figure's plinth is engraved with the name "Dagon," which is proceeded by a combination of marks that mean "progenitor" or "patriarch."

Take +1 **CLUE** and +1 **INTELLECT**, and the SECRET: *Hail Hydra.*

Turn to **252**.

243

Taking hold of a rusted iron handle each, between the two of you, you haul the chest out of the hole. You can't quite believe you have accomplished what Dr Addison set out to do – unearth the lost treasure of the pirate queen Mèng Yáo! At least you hope it's hers.

Take the Secret: *X Marks the Spot.*

You can only surmise that a previous landslide closed the entrance to this cave – after Mèng Yáo had buried her booty here – and that recent seismic activity has opened it up again.

But as you kneel in front of the chest, almost too afraid to open it, you feel a tremor pass through the ground that sets your heart racing, and the sharp crack of splintering rock echoes around the cavern.

Roll one die and add both your **COMBAT** and your **INTELLECT**. You may spend **1 RESOURCE** to roll two dice and pick the highest. You may also spend 1 clue and add 1 to the total. If you have the **{GUARDIAN}** or **{SURVIVOR}** Ability, add 1. If you have the **{CURSED}** or **{CLAUSTROPHOBIA}** Weakness, deduct 1. What's the result?

Total of 11 or more: turn to **279**.
10 or less: turn to **263**.

244

It may not be raining, but thanks to the clinging fog and the spray thrown up by the waves crashing against the shore below, the path down the face of the cliff is dangerously slippery.

When you do slip, you realize it was virtually inevitable. As your feet shoot out from under you, in a moment of scrabbling panic, you clutch at anything within reach in the hope of arresting your fall. And it works, but not before you are forced to confront the very real possibility that you could fall to your death at any moment, and this fact alone shakes you to your core. Take -1 **SANITY** and the Weakness **{FEAR OF HEIGHTS}**.

You manage to get to your feet again, despite the fact that your legs are shaking, and resume your descent.

Turn to **255**.

Trying to recall the details of Dr Addison's advert on the spot, you um and ah once too often, and your faltering explanation is not enough to convince the hotelier to hand over the room key. Perhaps you are not as well informed as you thought you were. Take -**1 INTELLECT**.

You only have two other options remaining to you.

> You can either wait in the hope that the old man will eventually have to leave his position at the front desk: turn to **56**.
> Or you can go back upstairs and try to force your way into Dr Addison's room: turn to **41**.

As you prepare to make a stand on the beach, you see three more hairless heads break the surface. You stare in horror at the creatures that are coming for you from the sea. They are humanoid in form, or simian at least, but their faces are fish-like, with great gaping mouths filled with pin-like teeth, while their bodies are covered with a layer of malformed scales. Their hands and feet are webbed and sport long claws.

As they leave the water, the creatures appear to gulp in air, while gill-like flaps in their necks rise and fall with the regularity of bellows.

Despite their clearly piscine appearance, the physiology of the fish-things still speaks of a human heritage, which is the most disturbing thing about their presence here. Take **-1 SANITY**.

You put up a valiant fight against the horrors from the deep, but Dr Addison has already abandoned you and it is not long before you are overwhelmed. One of the monsters clubs you on the side of the head with a scaled fist and you hit the sand hard. As consciousness fades, you hear a cry and know that the fish-men have caught up with the academic as well.

Take **-2 HEALTH** and **-1 COMBAT**.

Roll one die and deduct 1 if you have the **{SURVIVOR}** or **{TOUGH}** Ability.

> If the total is equal to or less than your **HEALTH**, turn to **298**.
> If the total is greater than your **HEALTH**, turn to **13**.

247

As you prepare to make a stand, you cannot hide the revulsion you feel in the presence of such malformed hybrids. They are ape-like in form, but their faces are fish-like, with great gaping mouths filled with needle-sharp teeth, while their bodies are covered with a layer of chitinous scales. Their hands and feet are webbed and sport long claws.

Despite looking like they would be more at home under the sea, the creatures are taking in great gulps of air, while gill-like flaps in their necks rise and fall with the regularity of bellows. And there is still something about the physiology of the horrors that speaks of a distant human heritage, which is almost more disturbing than their grotesque appearance. Take -**1 SANITY**.

You put up a valiant fight against the creatures, but Dr Addison has already abandoned you and it is not long before you are overwhelmed. One of the monsters clubs you on the side of the head with a scaled fist and you hit the ground hard. As consciousness fades, you hear a cry and know that the fish-men have caught up with the academic as well.

Take -**2 HEALTH** and -**1 COMBAT**.

Roll one die and deduct 1 if you have the **{SURVIVOR}** or **{TOUGH}** Ability.

> If the total is equal to or less than your **HEALTH**, turn to **298**.
> If the total is greater than your **HEALTH**, turn to **13**.

248

"How do you mean 'gone missing'?" you ask.

"I mean that they were here one day, they checked into the hotel, and then no one ever saw them again."

"That doesn't necessarily mean anything untoward happened to them. It could have simply been that no one saw them leave."

"Very well then," Brian goes on. "Have you seen any of the locals up close?"

"Aren't you local?" you ask.

"I'm from Arkham," the young man explains. "I board with a family from Ipswich and go back home whenever I get a moment off. My family does not like me working in Innsmouth, but I've invested a lot of time and money in this store and do not wish to give up my job just yet. Besides, the townsfolk seem to have accepted me and rely on what I can offer them." He takes in the stacked shelves with the sweep of an arm. "But anyone else they find snooping around had best watch out."

"Why?"

"You've seen them, haven't you?" He gives an involuntary shiver. "Those staring, unblinking eyes? And their voices are no more than disgusting gargles. It is awful to hear them chanting in their churches at night, and especially during their main festivals, which fall on April 30 and October 31."

You are certainly less keen to remain in Innsmouth overnight after speaking with the young entrepreneur. Take **+1 CLUE** and **-1 SANITY**.

Turn to **259**.

249

The cottage is in darkness. Trying the door, you find that it is locked. You see that a **[SPADE]** has been left propped against the wall of the cottage. You ponder whether you should spare the time to pick it up. If you do take the **[SPADE]**, record it on your Character Sheet and take **+1 RESOURCE.**

"Come on!" Dr Addison shouts at you, her voice faint. "This isn't getting us any closer to finding the treasure. Let's go!"

You certainly don't feel like you want to remain here any longer than necessary, and the thought of finding the long-lost treasure of Mèng Yáo helps convince you that Dr Addison is right.

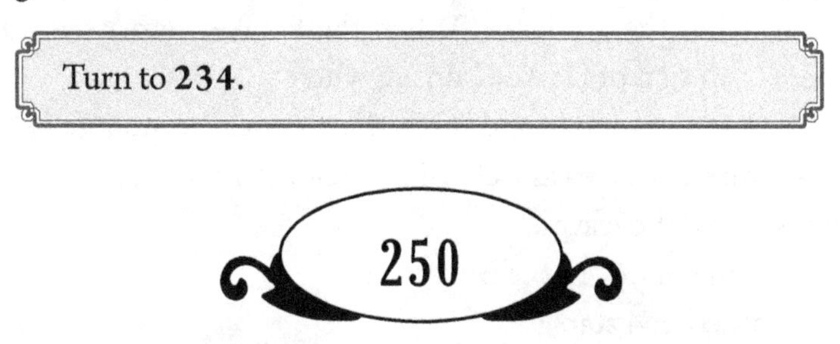

Turn to **234**.

250

The first thing you are going to have to do is scale the cliff face, negotiating the steep, narrow path that leads from the bottom to the top. But you are exhausted and every step feels like you are trudging through a swamp.

Halfway to the top you almost lose consciousness as the world spins around you. Recent events have taken a heavy toll not just on your body but your mind as well.

"Give me the statue," Dr Addison says, her voice as mellifluous as a hot toddy. "You are clearly exhausted. Let me carry that burden for a bit."

You reluctantly agree and pass the [GREENSTONE STATUE] to the academic. Strike the [GREENSTONE STATUE] from your Character Sheet. Almost immediately, you feel your head start to clear and are filled with a renewed vigor to continue the climb.

Despite the leviathan monster being big and powerful enough to kill a whale with its bare hands, the effigy still exerts an influence over the sea monster, holding both it and its brood at bay.

Then the unthinkable happens. One moment, Dr Addison is climbing the path behind you, the next you hear a stifled gasp of shock and turn in time to see her death-plunge down the face of the cliff. But before her body can be smashed on the boulders below, a great wave sweeps in off the sea – sending up a great wall of spray as it strikes the wall of rock – and catches the academic. When the breaker retreats again, there is no sign of Dr Addison anywhere.

With the academic and the artifact gone, the strange fish-folk return to the sea as well, while their monstrous progenitor sinks below the waves.

Take the SECRET: *The Hungry Sea.*

Final score: 4 stars.

Turn to **300**.

251

A crate has been left at the juncture where the wall protrudes at right angles from the canning plant. Climbing onto this, you then use a drainpipe to aid your attempt to scale the wall. But whether you are successful or not will depend on your upper body strength.

Roll one die and deduct 1 if you have the **{AGILE}** Ability.

> If the total is equal to or less than your **HEALTH**, turn to **38**.
> If the total is greater than your **HEALTH**, turn to **8**.

252

Reaching the rocky ledge, you clamber out of the water, dripping wet, but you do not stop to wring out your clothes or even empty the seawater from your boots. You have no desire to remain here a moment longer and make for the tunnel mouth.

But as you are entering the fissure in the rock, you imagine you hear something, like a splash or the echo of a water droplet entering the pool. You turn, just for a moment, giving the silent, motionless figures one last glance before departing this place for good.

If you have the **{PARANOID}** Weakness, take **-1 SANITY**.

> Turn to **136**.

253

The atmosphere you felt at the Innsmouth Jail made you uncomfortable. You're certainly not prepared to take the police force of this town at their word. You need to find Dr Addison yourself, and fast. Spend either 1 clue or 1 resource or take +**1 DOOM**.

But as you make your way through the town, you feel eyes on you everywhere you go. Are you going mad or are the curious townsfolk really spying on you?

> If you have the Weakness **{WATCHED}**, turn to **7**.
> If not, turn to **34**.

254

Your pace quickens as you head in what you think is the direction of the river, hoping to follow that watercourse to the Town Square.

Not only are you unable to shake the feeling that your every move is being watched by bulging, unblinking eyes, but now you are even starting to imagine you can hear exchanges in an utterly inhuman, gurgling, croaking tongue, emanating from behind closed doors.

Why did you ever dare to visit Innsmouth in the first place? Take -**1 WILLPOWER** and -**1 SANITY**.

> Turn to **187**.

255

Progress is slow but steady and you eventually make it to the bottom. Looking back up at that imposing wall of rock, you can hardly believe you made it down in one piece.

Somewhere beneath this headland lies the lost treasure of Mèng Yáo the pirate queen. And so, you set off across the stony beach, scouring the cliff face for fissures that could be cave entrances.

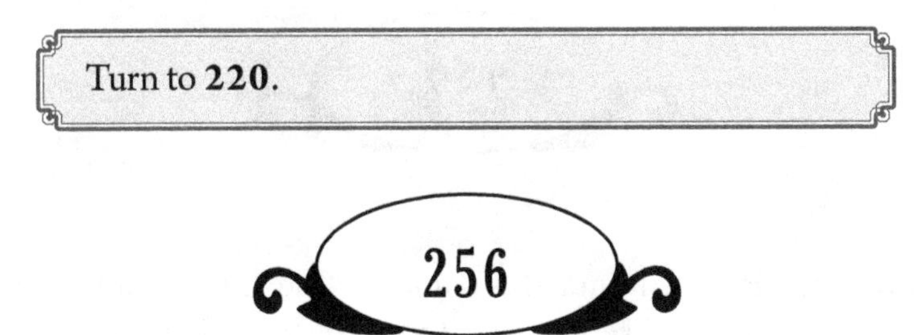

Turn to **220**.

256

As Dr Addison catches up with you, not knowing what else to do, you snatch the grotesque figurine from the academic's hands – even as she utters a vehement protest – and you hold it up before the advancing horrors.

"Give that back to me!" Dr Addison screams, clawing at your arm and hand holding the **[GREENSTONE STATUE]**.

But then, as one, the fish-folk come to an immediate stop, all eyes on the idol held tightly in your hand. As you suspected, it is either of immense value to them and they do not want to do anything that could result in it being damaged, or it actually has some strange hold over them. Or both.

But it isn't only the deep-dwellers that can feel the dark power exuded by the effigy working within them. You can feel it too. Waves of what feels like a malignant intelligence wash over you, breaking down your resistance and threatening to supplant your own consciousness.

Make a fate test. Roll one die, and if you have the Weakness {**CURSED**} or {**TROUBLED DREAMS**}, deduct 1.

> If the result is equal to or lower than the current doom level, turn to **205**.
> If not, turn to **185**.

257

Considering you found the name of The Little Bookshop written down in [**DR ADDISON'S DIARY**], it's possible she visited this place before you. And if she did, perhaps Joyce knows where she is now.

And then there was Addison's reference to the tidal tunnels. Although it seems unlikely, could the academic have come here to find out more about the tunnels, specifically, or maybe even the wreck of the pirate junk?

What do you want to do?

> Ask if Joyce can tell you anything about the tidal tunnels: turn to **287**.
> Ask her about local shipwrecks: turn to **277**.
> Ask her about Dr Addison: turn to **25**.
> Leave The Little Bookshop without asking its proprietor anything: turn to **35**.

258

The pale-faced humanoid creature reaches for you with hands that are as white as alabaster, the skin wrinkled as if they have been submerged in water for an excessively long time. Despite feeling repulsed by his unsettling appearance, you nonetheless prepare to incapacitate the priest so he can do nothing to obstruct your flight from this unholy place, wherever it is.

You may spend **1 RESOURCE** at the start of each round to add 2 to your total for that round.

Round one: roll two dice and add your **COMBAT** and your **WILLPOWER**. If you have the **{SORCERY}** Ability, add 1. If the total is 15 or more, you win the first round.

Round two: roll two dice and add your **COMBAT** and your **WILLPOWER**. If you have the **{SORCERY}** Ability, add 1. If you won the first round, add 2. If your total is 16 or more, you win the second round.

If you won the second round, turn to **228**.
If you lost the second round, turn to **218**.

259

"But if one was determined to remain here and explore," you say, "what would it be useful to know?"

Brian looks at you uncertainly, then smooths out a piece of paper he would normally use to wrap someone's sausages and, producing a pencil from behind his ear, starts to sketch a map of the town.

"You could head out along the breakwater," he says as he deftly draws the harbor in aerial view. "You'll get a good view of Devil Reef from there, sea and fog willing, but the lighthouse at the end fell into ruin years ago. Heading into town, there are a few shops you might like to visit. Sightseers will find plenty to marvel at in Henderson's Oddities, and The Little Bookshop is worth a visit too." He marks these places on the map for you. "But whatever you do, steer clear of the cannery" – he circles a spot close to where the Manuxet River pours into Innsmouth Bay – "and certainly don't enter the slums that surround the Marsh Refinery." He points out another place on the map with his pencil before putting a large X through it. "They don't like strangers visiting that part of town."

He hastily shoves the map into your hands as one of the fish-faced townspeople approaches the till. Take **+2 CLUES.**

"But like I said," he hisses, "you do not want to be here after dark!"

You feel obliged to the young Brian Burnham for his assistance and wonder if there is some practical way you could demonstrate your gratitude.

If you would like to buy something from the store before you leave, turn to **270.**
If you would rather leave and make your way to the Gilman House Hotel for your meeting with Dr Addison, turn to **83.**

260

Your opponent staggers and falls, and a gust of foul-smelling breath escapes whatever passes for lungs within the monster's physiology.

If you want to press home the advantage and drive the other horrors from the beach, turn to **286.**
If you think a change of plan might be a better course of action, turn to **256.**

Even though you give the entrance to the canning plant a wide berth, you can't help feeling that the goons on guard are watching you. If you have the Weakness **{PARANOID}**, take -**1 WILLPOWER**.

Rounding the corner of the great shed, you lose sight of the sentries and, farther on still, come to an enclosure surrounded by a high brick wall that projects from the northern side of the plant. There does not appear to be anyone on guard here and this spot is overlooked by nothing more that the empty windows of abandoned buildings.

Passing the walled yard, you find yourself by the harbor's water edge and within easy reach of the slipway that projects from the eastern end of the cannery.

So, you have two options available by which you could hopefully gain access to the factory unseen.

To try to climb over the wall, turn to **251**.
To gain access via the slipway, turn to **18**.
If you no longer want to gain access to the cannery, turn to **28**.

262

You can barely believe what is now standing there, right before your eyes. It is like something out of a nightmare, an impossible amalgamation of sea-dweller and man, but its sharp claws and pointed teeth, not to mention its aggressive attitude, seem all too real.

You may spend **1 RESOURCE** at the start of each round to add 2 to your total for that round.

Round one: roll two dice and add your **COMBAT**. If you have the Weakness **{HAUNTED}**, deduct 2. If you have the **{TOUGH}** Ability, add 1. If the total is 12 or more, you win the first round.

Round two: roll two dice and add your **COMBAT**. If you have the Weakness **{HAUNTED}**, deduct 2. If you have the **{FIGHTER}** Ability, add 1. If you won the first round, add 2. If your total is 13 or more, you win the second round.

If you won the second round, turn to **282**.
If you lost the second round, turn to **272**.

A chunk of rock breaks free of the ceiling and plummets to the ground, but you only realize you are directly under it when there's barely time to do anything about it. You attempt to roll out of the way, but the shard still slices a nasty gash in your arm as it buries itself in the hole you've just excavated. Take -**1 HEALTH** and -**1 COMBAT**.

Turn to **289**.

"I wouldn't do that if I were you," Dr Addison throws back, realizing what you are intending as you reach for the chest. "Have you not heard of pirate curses? Leave it where it is or incur the wrath of Mèng Yáo herself."

If you want to take some of the gold despite Dr Addison's warning, turn to **55**.
If you think it wiser to heed her advice, turn to **137**.

265

You tell him that Dr Addison is researching shipwrecks in the area and you are helping her with her latest investigation. You explain that the two of you are colleagues, exaggerating how well you know the academic and how important your role is, telling him that you have journeyed some way to get here and would really appreciate the chance to freshen up in her room.

Apparently satisfied with your explanation, the manager hands you the key. You waste no time in going back upstairs and letting yourself into Room #428.

Turn to **235**.

266

The cottage is in darkness. As you approach you can see no sign of anyone being at home. Either that or whoever lives there doesn't find their vision hampered by a lack of light. However, you do find a **[SPADE]** propped against the wall outside the door. If you take the **[SPADE]**, record it on your Character Sheet and take **+1 RESOURCE**.

But then your attention is taken by a light bobbing through the gloom.

"What's that?" Dr Addison hisses, joining you in pressing her back up against the wall of the cottage, hoping to hide herself in the shadows.

You watch the light for a moment. It is hard to be sure, but it appears to be moving away from the cottage and toward the lighthouse. It reminds you of an anglerfish's bobbing, bioluminescent lure.

"It's moving away from us, whatever it is. I'm sure of it."

"Come on," says your companion, "this isn't getting us any closer to finding the treasure. We should get back to the cliff."

If you want to head to the cliff as Dr Addison suggests, turn to **99**.

If you would rather head toward the lighthouse together, turn to **154**.

Perhaps the academic visited The Little Bookshop with the intention of perusing the local history section, hoping to find some useful tidbit related to her quest to discover the wreck of the pirate ship.

If so, perhaps Joyce spoke with Dr Addison. And if that is the case, then maybe she knows where the doctor is now.

If you want to ask Joyce if she knows anything about local shipwrecks, turn to **277**.

If you want to ask her about Dr Addison, turn to **25**.

If you would rather leave The Little Bookshop without asking her anything, turn to **35**.

268

All your suppressed fear and panic is suddenly released in an adrenaline-fueled burst of energy that has you taking flight through the building. With Dr Addison at your side, you both run to the end of the corridor and down a staircase until you find yourselves in a grand hallway. It is decorated with all manner of unnerving exhibits that only spur you on to find a way out of this place. But you are not out of danger yet.

You can hear feet slapping on the stairs behind you as the beings who worship here chase after you and the fleeing Dr Addison.

Perhaps simply fleeing is not enough.

To turn and prepare to challenge your pursuers, turn to **116**.
To take something from your pack to use against them, turn to **93**.
To rampage through the hall, tearing down some of the exhibits as you go, turn to **284**.

269

Before the lighthouse keeper has a chance to secure the door behind him, you burst through it. You find yourself in a nondescript chamber of whitewashed stone, with stairs curving around the inner wall of the structure leading both up to the light and down to a basement.

As you stand inside the door trying to decide which way your quarry went, something heavy crashes down on top of your head. The lighthouse keeper was waiting for you, unseen behind the door.

You lose consciousness, never to wake again, so, fortunately, you do not discover the fate that Oceiros Marsh and his warped kin have in store for you.

The End.

270

You purchase an innocuous sandwich and a bottle of root beer. Take +**1 RESOURCE**.

You pay the young man and the till rings, signaling it is time for you to leave the First National Grocery. Despite all that Brian Burnham has told you, you are determined to at least meet with Dr Addison, having made the effort to travel to this dilapidated seaside town.

Turn to **83**.

271

As you stride purposefully toward the entrance, the goons move to block your passage.

"What do you want?" one of them growls, while his companion cracks his knuckles emphatically.

If you have the {SAILOR} Ability, turn to **119**.
If not, turn to **109**.

272

The creature seizes you in a bear hug and without a moment's pause, throws itself back into the water. Taken by surprise, you barely have time to take a breath before the horror is dragging you deeper and deeper into the seemingly bottomless pool.

Your ears pop and your lungs begin to burn. Your eyes sting from the saltwater and all you can see is the grotesque, anglerfish-like face of the creature that has you in its cruel grasp.

You get the sense that you have left the semi-flooded tidal tunnels far behind and are now heading out into the open sea. And there, in the distance through the gloom, you fancy you can see the flicker of bioluminescence outlining colossal structures that look like sunken palaces, towers, and cathedrals buried beneath – or perhaps even formed from – accretions of coral.

And then you can hold your breath no longer.

They say that after the initial shock, drowning is a relatively peaceful way to die, but you do so staring into the grisly visage of the fish-thing, a horror that thankfully most will never have to face.

The End.

"Why are you really here?" the deputy constable challenges you.

And then, without giving you a chance to answer his question, he launches into an apparently heartfelt tirade of vitriol.

"I know your type. People like you only come here to make trouble. No one just happens to visit Innsmouth. Everyone who comes here from outside does so to spy on good, honest, hardworking folk and look for cock-and-bull stories about town worthies like the Marsh family. I think it's time you left before I arrest you for wasting police time. Now, be on your way."

If you want to leave quietly, turn to **293**.
If you want to demand to speak to Deputy Constable Ropes' superior, turn to **207**.

Keeping out of reach of the cultists' grasping hands, you burst out of the room. Dr Addison runs with you to the end of the corridor and you descend the stone staircase that awaits you there.

The relief you feel upon finally exiting the building is palpable, and you throw yourself down the steps outside the former Masonic Hall, which now bears the name of the Esoteric Order of Dagon. But you are not out of danger yet.

You can hear the bare feet of the members of the Esoteric Order slapping on the stones of the steps as they chase after you and Dr Addison, who is already some yards ahead.

Turn to **200**.

As you had hoped, the wood around the lock splinters and you half-stumble into the room beyond.

Turn to **235**.

276

Do you have any idea where the lost treasure of Mèng Yáo might be buried?

If so, turn the letters in the two-word name of the location (ignoring the definite article) into numbers, using the code A=1, B=2… Z=26, add all the numbers together, and then turn to the same section as the sum.

A	B	C	D	E	F	G	H	I	J
1	2	3	4	5	6	7	8	9	10
K	**L**	**M**	**N**	**O**	**P**	**Q**	**R**	**S**	**T**
11	12	13	14	15	16	17	18	19	20
U	**V**	**W**	**X**	**Y**	**Z**				
21	22	23	24	25	26				

If the section makes no sense, either you have made a mistake in your adding up or you are wrong in your assumption. If there is somewhere else you know of that you could try, repeat the process outlined above.

If you end up at a dead end but have both the [TREASURE HUNTER'S CHART] and a [LOGBOOK], turn to **182**.

If you have just one of these items, turn to **166**.

If you do not have either of these things, turn to **17**.

277

"Well, the shore along this stretch of coast is certainly treacherous, festooned with jagged rocks," Joyce replies. "Many a ship has fallen foul of the hidden reefs that lie just under the surface in the bay. Is there a particular wreck you are interested in?"

Unfortunately, you only know that it is that of a pirate ship, specifically a junk, but you can't tell her any more than that.

"A pirate ship, you say? How very Boy's Own Paper. That said, I do recall reading about the legend of a pirate ship in V.C. Creighton's Old Wrecks of New England. I don't know what it was called, but it was supposed to have gone down with all hands close to Falcon Point – that's another settlement south of here. Rumor has it that it was carrying a hold full of treasure pillaged from the South China Sea. Sorry I can't be of any more help than that."

Take +**1 CLUE** and the SECRET: *With All Hands.*

What do you want to do now?

If you want to ask Joyce about Dr Addison, turn to **25**.

If you would rather leave The Little Bookshop and look elsewhere for information regarding the academic's whereabouts, turn to **35**.

278

Making your way to the door to the left, lured by the light, you find yourself at the entrance to what would appear to be a robing room, like that of some Masonic lodge.f

Dr Addison waits in the corridor, hissing that you need to hurry, but your gaze is drawn to an ornate headpiece – like a diadem or crown – resting on a turquoise velvet cushion. At first glance you would say that it is made of gold, but as you approach, the light reflecting from it shifts. It seems possessed of an additional lustrous quality that ripples across its surface like sunlight underwater.

The design of the piece is something else altogether. It is made up of various coils that intertwine with each other so that when it is worn, the whole looks like an octopus wrapped around the wearer's head.

So taken are you by the artifact that you do not notice the other occupant of the room until he turns from the open wardrobe in which his robes of office are kept, having just put them on. He is a bald man, with skin the color of a mackerel's belly and drooping, wide-set watery eyes. His aquamarine and gold robes make him look like the priest of some pagan cult, but one with a taste for opulent outfits.

You stare at each other for a moment, both taken aback, his sagging mouth opening and closing like that of an overgrown carp.

A gurgling cry rises from the pallid priest's throat, snapping you out of your reverie, and you realize he is calling for help!

How do you want to respond?

Turn tail and run: turn to **268**.
Attack the priest before any reinforcements can arrive: turn to **258**.
Snatch the curious crown: turn to **238**.

Your instincts do not fail you, and you spot exactly where the danger lies and roll out of the way as a chunk of rock breaks free of the ceiling and plummets to the ground, burying itself in the hole you've just excavated.

"That was close," Dr Addison gasps with obvious relief.

"But what caused it?" you reply.

"The tremor, clearly," the academic snaps.

"That's what I was talking about," you explain. "What is causing the tremors?"

Turn to **289**.

You cast your eyes toward the ramshackle jetty. Your boat is still tied up there, riding the wash that continually batters its hull.

As if reading your mind, Dr Addison says, "No, we stay on the land."

"But we will be able to travel much more quickly by boat than on foot," you point out.

"But the sea is their domain," your companion replies, turning her attention from the boat back to the creatures standing amidst the breakers.

What do you think?

> If you want to make your getaway by boat, turn to **150**.
> If you want to flee on foot and keep to the land, turn to **250**.

In its heyday, Innsmouth was at the heart of shipbuilding in New England. But with the decline the town has suffered over the last hundred years or more, the vast shipyards and colossal warehouses now stand vacant and derelict.

However, the Innsmouth Cannery is a relatively recent development that has taken over a huge barn-like shed on the northern edge of the harbor. It is a large, rectangular, brick-built structure accessed through a fenced compound that faces away from the sea. The cannery also projects out into the harbor itself. At this end of the building, a barnacle-covered slipway connects a cavernous unloading bay to the torpid, weed-choked waters. The pilings on which the cannery and the slipway are supported are sunk into the harbor's mud that is exposed at low tide.

As you approach the cannery, you can hear the clanking of machinery operating within and smoke billows from a tall brick chimney. Two sullen-looking individuals swathed in heavy coats and woolen sweaters, their faces hidden under peaked caps, stand at the fenced compound entrance, watching the workers who are passing in and out of the plant.

If you really suspect that Dr Addison might be somewhere inside the weather-boarded building, or that someone working there might know where she is, you are going to have to pluck up the courage to choose a way in.

> If you want to approach the obvious entrance to the cannery, turn to **271**.
> If you want to find another way in, turn to **261**.
> If you have changed your mind about visiting the cannery, turn to **28**.

You manage to bind the creature's hands in your own. In frustration, it snaps at your face with its great, shark-like teeth, but you pull your head back out of the way. With one swift movement, you release your hold on the thing and grab its head instead, forcing a thumb into one of its bulging white eyes.

You hear a horrible yet satisfying pop, and with a shriek of pain, the creature breaks off its attack and throws itself back into the pool.

Not waiting to see if it will surface again, you flee from the cave.

Turn to **136**.

"Devil Reef?" you say.

"Thar's whar it all begun, that cursed place of all wickedness whar the deep water starts," the old man replies. "Gate o' hell – sheer drop daown to a bottom no saoundin'-line kin tech. Ol' Cap'n Obed done it – him that faound aout more'n was good fer him in the Saouth Sea islands."

What would make the old man describe the reef as a gateway to hell?

You listen as the old man continues his tale, although it is quite hard to follow. There is talk of young men going missing from the town, gunshots heard out on the reef, and an invasion of creatures from the sea. As far as you can work out, this all happened decades ago, possibly around the time the strange plague struck the town.

You have no idea how much, if any, of the old man's tale is true, but it unsettles you to be sure. Take -**1 SANITY**, +**1 CLUE**, and the SECRET: *Old Sea Dogs' Tales.*

"Folks aoutside hev their stories abaout us," the old man goes on. "S'pose you've heerd a plenty on 'em – stories abaout that strange joolry as comes in from somewhars an' ain't quite all melted up. They call 'em gold-like things pirate loot, an' say the Innsmouth folks is distempered or somethin'. Besides, them that lives here shoo off as many strangers as they kin, an' encourage the rest not to git very cur'ous, specially raound nighttime."

At this, the old man takes something from his coat pocket and hands it to you. It is an old **[SHIP'S COMPASS]**.

"If you's the cur'ous kind, this'll see you right."

Turn to **294**.

Seizing hold of a marble bust, you hurl it to the floor, where it shatters into a thousand pieces. A cry goes up from the cultists, but they falter in their advance. Spurred on by their reaction, you grab hold of a glass cabinet and send that crashing to the ground as well.

Feeling that you have probably done enough to delay the cultists' pursuit, you head for the exit. Take **+1 INTELLECT**.

The relief you feel upon finally exiting the building is palpable, and you throw yourself down the steps outside the former Masonic Hall that now bears the name the Esoteric Order of Dagon. But you are not out of danger yet.

You can hear the bare feet of the members of the Esoteric Order slapping on the stones of the steps as they chase after you and Dr Addison, who is already some yards ahead.

Turn to **200**.

285

The door panels give slightly under the impact, but the lock remains intact. You try again.

You bounce off the resisting wood, but this time hear a sharp splintering sound. Encouraged, you charge the door for a third time.

With a crash, you burst through it into the room beyond but wince at the sharp pain you feel in your shoulder as a consequence. Take **-1 HEALTH**.

Turn to **235**.

You put up a brave defense, but there are simply too many monsters. And where one falls there are always three more ready to take its place.

You are soon overwhelmed. While you may be incapacitated, you are still alive when the horrors begin to feed. Take the SECRET: *Wish You Were Here?*

The End.

"I've heard that Innsmouth is built on top of a network of caves and that the tunnels that lead below ground are only revealed at low tide. Can you tell me any more about them?"

"No," the woman says flatly, her previously open demeanor replaced by one of, if not outright hostility, then at least curt unfriendliness.

"I guess it's possible that the cellars of some of the older properties could even connect to those tunnels," you go on, unable to help yourself. "I don't suppose the basement of your bookshop is like that, is it?"

"I don't know what really brought you to Innsmouth, but you won't find it here." Joyce spits out the words. "I think it's time you left. Good day!"

For a moment you consider challenging the woman's outright refusal to discuss the subject of the tidal tunnels, but when you think about it, you don't know what it would achieve. Besides, her cold gaze is making you uneasy.

Without saying another word, you exit The Little Bookshop. Take -1 **WILLPOWER**.

Turn to **35**.

288

The locals know to avoid this place, but in your distracted state you have walked into more trouble than you can handle. You manage to disarm one of the thugs, but his friend slashes at you with his knife, catching your arm and drawing blood. Take -1 **HEALTH** and -1 **COMBAT**.

Seeing an opportunity, and having no other choice, you break from the fight and flee back along Sawbone Alley.

You get the feeling that if you are being hunted after making enquiries about the whereabouts of Dr Addison, then she must be in trouble. You need to find her before it's too late!

Turn to **34**.

Able to contain herself no longer, Dr Addison tries the lid of the chest, finds it unlocked – or the lock rusted away – and eases it open.

You are unable to hide your amazement and gasp as you set eyes upon the lost treasure of the Golden Breeze. There are some doubloons and even a golden necklace set with semi-precious stones, but much of the cache consists of pieces of a gold-like substance with a lustrous sheen that have been fashioned into esoteric pieces of jewelry.

Dr Addison plunges her hands into the chest and swirls the treasure between her figures until she finds what she is looking for and pulls out a curious totemic figure carved from a milky-green stone that could be jade, although you're not sure.

"I was right!" Dr Addison exclaims. She is the most animated you have seen her. "To have in my hands something from lost Atlantis..." For a moment she is lost for words, and you can even see tears in her eyes as she whispers, "Now Dagon will answer to Asturias."

Whilst clearly being primitive in form and ancient in origin, the effigy puts you in mind of a creature that is equal parts man and fish and yet, at the same time, neither. It is squatting on a base inscribed with strange runic symbols, three rows of five on each of its four sides.

"If this really did come from Atlantis," you say, transfixed by the unsettling idol, "how did it end up in the possession of the pirate queen?"

"Mèng Yáo acquired it when she and her crew ran aground on a previously unknown island in the Pacific," the academic says, her voice having acquired a dreamy quality. "When the pirates fled this curious island, pursued by deep-dwellers like those we have already encountered, the pirate queen was able to use the idol to hold them back. And when she learned what had happened following Obed Marsh's time in Polynesia, she traveled here, intending to use the idol to deal with the cult of Dagon herself. But her junk sank off the coast of Massachusetts in a terrible storm. She and a handful of her men managed to escape and hide the treasure before the fish-worshippers found them."

"And this is where they hid it," you say, taking in your surrounding with new eyes. You can imagine what happened next; the cave was sealed by a cave-in as the waves lashed the cliffs of Falcon Point, and Mèng Yáo and her men drowned.

"Only one of her crew managed to escape, barely alive," Dr Addison goes on. "Rescued by a merchant ship, before he died, he told the sailors his strange story, and so the legend of the pirate queen Mèng Yáo and her cursed treasure was born. And now it is mine."

The [GREENSTONE STATUE] in hand, Dr Addison turns on her heel and heads for the way out of the cave again.

"Is that all you wanted?" you challenge her. "What about the rest of the treasure? What about the gold?"

"I've got what I came here for," replies the academic. "There is nothing more valuable. You helped me find it and for that I thank you. Now, are you coming or not?"

You must be staring at a fortune in pirate booty, but there's no way you can drag the chest out of here by yourself. So, what do you want to do?

If you want to fill your pockets with gold, turn to **264**.
If you would rather leave the cave before any more of the roof can come down, turn to **178**.

290

Crossing Main Street you follow the road, not to mention the smell of seafood, until you find yourself on Fish Street. Compared to the other thoroughfares you have traveled along since arriving in Innsmouth, this is the first fully paved street you have come across. Despite that, it is still like a place stuck in the past, for the only traffic you can immediately see on the road either goes by foot or horsedrawn wagon. Nonetheless, you do come across the occasional battered motorcar pulled up next to the curb. Farther along the road you can see a series of desultory market stalls from which the local fishing families are selling the day's catch.

With so much seafood on offer and apparently so few people around to buy it, you are not surprised to stumble upon a streetside café offering all manner of freshly caught and cooked fish on its menu board.

As you enter the eatery, the woman behind the counter offers you an insipid smile whilst studying you with a watery, barely blinking gaze. Today's offerings are displayed on mounds of crushed ice and while many of them are things you don't recognize, you pick out a fine Atlantic cod, which is brought to your table within half an hour, served with a side order of desultory vegetables. The fish is delicious but everything else has been boiled to a virtual mush and you leave much of it untouched on the side of your plate. Take **+1 HEALTH** and **+1 DOOM**.

Having eaten your fill and paid the bill, you make your way back to the Town Square, eager to meet with Dr Addison and find out precisely what it is you have signed yourself up for.

Turn to **83**.

291

"It's working!" Dr Addison says in a harsh whisper at your shoulder. "The idol is holding them at bay."

"So, what do we do now?" you grunt through gritted teeth.

"Now we get out of here," comes her terse reply. "As fast as we can."

> If you have the {**SAILOR**} Ability, turn to **280**.
> If not, turn to **250**.

292

The town has become so run down that one sagging street front looks very much like the next, with little in the way of distinctive landmarks, other than the crumbling church towers, to aid your navigation of the town.

Wherever you wander, you feel the eyes of the local populace upon you and the more you begin to feel that you are not safe here. When a huddle of men – their faces all bearing the same "Innsmouth look," with unblinking eyes, wide mouths with flabby lips and sagging jowls – break off their gurgling conversation and start to approach you, you duck down a side street to avoid a confrontation. You attempt to turn back in what you think is the direction of the Town Square but soon find yourself lost in the warren of streets north of the river that border the harbor instead.

A malodorous miasma hangs over this part of the town. You soon discover the source of the stomach-turning stench: the streets are littered with the liquifying remains of fish and other sea creatures hauled up from the deep in the fishermen's nets. The waters off Innsmouth must be rich indeed for so much of their catch to be left to rot like this among the broken cobbles and brackish puddles.

Gulls watch you from the rooftops or where they are picking at bits of suckered tentacle in the street, their keening cries occasionally cutting through the biting salt-sea air.

You do not feel safe at all and begin to imagine all manner of inhuman things are watching you from gaps in the boarded-up windows and cloth-draped doorways of the moldering tenements. You have to get out of here and fast!

Roll one die, and if you have either the **{CURSED}** or **{HAUNTED}** Weakness, add 1.

If the total is equal to or less than your **SANITY**, turn to **187**.
If the total is greater than your sanity, turn to **254**.

You feel that you have stirred up a viper nest by coming here and so leave again without having to be asked twice, fearful of what might happen if you don't.

Take -1 **WILLPOWER** and gain the Weakness {**WATCHED**}, if you don't already have it.

Turn to **253**.

Feeling eyes boring into your back, you scour the harbor and see a gang of fishermen watching you with a steely intensity, from where they are sat amidst a stack of barnacled lobster pots. They all have the same uncanny look about them – drooping eyes, pale skin, and a noticeable lack of facial hair.

You know when you're not welcome. Lingering here any longer, at this time, would benefit no one, least of all you. Spend either 1 clue or 1 resource or take +1 **DOOM**.

So, where do you want to go to continue your investigation, away from the prying eyes of the fishermen?

Henderson's Oddities: turn to **45**.
The Little Bookshop: turn to **91**.
Down to the shore: turn to **126**.
The Innsmouth Cannery: turn to **281**.
If there is an alternative location you would like to visit, turn to **170**.

295

Taking a firm hold of the handle you slam your shoulder into the door, hoping that the force of the impact will splinter the wood around the lock.

Roll one die and add your **COMBAT**. If you have the **{TOUGH}** Ability, add 1. What's the total?

8 or more: turn to **275**.
7 or less: turn to **285**.

296

As you make your way across the scrubby ground toward the lighthouse, the fog closes in again. Objects that were at least partially visible before become instinct shadows within the murk, which takes on a jaundiced hue in the presence of the sweeping beacon.

Sounds also become changed by the fog, so that you cannot be certain from whence they came. So, when you hear a foghorn-like bellow, it has you scanning the mist all around you, the primal fear that makes the hairs on the back of your neck stand on end driving you to determine where the next threat to your life might come from.

Was it a ship warning others of its presence in the thickening fog? Or was it of animal origin? Take **-1 SANITY**.

Your attention is suddenly stolen by something much closer to hand. A light is bobbing through the darkness, like some supernatural will-o'-the-wisp. But there's no marsh up here on the headland, and therefore no emissions of gases produced by organic decay to cause photon emissions.

You watch the moving light for a moment as it dances around the base of the lighthouse, until it disappears again moments later.

Turn to **154**.

297

Homing in on the source of the splashing, you crouch and find yourself staring into a water-filled crevice in the rock, in which an octopus appears to have become trapped. Only you're not sure it is an octopus. There is something of the jellyfish about it as well. It's certainly nothing you recognize.

As you are considering the creature, a gelatinous arm whips out of the water, its tip catching you on the back of the hand. You immediately cry out in pain and pull your hand away as it becomes the focus of an intense burning sensation. As you watch, the skin becomes inflamed and covered with a rash of welts.

The agony is like nothing you've ever known and even though it begins to diminish after a few minutes, it doesn't go away entirely and remains an uncomfortable distraction. Take **-1 HEALTH**, **-1 COMBAT**, and **-1 WILLPOWER**. Spend either **1 CLUE** or **1 RESOURCE** or take **+1 DOOM**.

You've definitely had enough of poking about this wretched place now.

Turn to **28**.

You wake to darkness and a bump the size of an egg on the back of your head. You are lying on a cold marble floor, so you sit up and immediately regret the decision as you are beset by a splitting headache, and a wave of nausea churns your stomach.

You flop back onto the floor and it is then that you realize your wrists have been tied behind your back. Your ankles have been bound, too. A groan of discomfort escapes your lips and is answered by another groan from beside you.

Blinking, you peer into the near darkness and see shapes start to resolve as your eyes become accustomed to the gloom. There are no details, only shapes, and the closest of those is Dr Addison. You have both been taken prisoner and brought to this place – wherever this place is – but for what purpose you dread to think. If a certain segment of the local populace didn't want you sticking your nose into their affairs, why keep you alive at all?

There are windows in this room but all you can see through them is an oily darkness and strands of jaundiced fog.

With your vision dramatically impaired by the lack of light, you focus on your other senses to see what you can learn. The air is redolent with curious scents, a strange mélange of incense and damp, but it lacks the salty tang of the ocean. While the chamber you have been left in is quiet, it is not silent; you can hear the faint echo of gargling voices coming from somewhere nearby.

As you strain to make out distinct words and phrases, you hear the ringing of approaching footsteps; yellow light abruptly finds its way into the room, and the black silhouette of a figure enters the chamber.

Fearing what might be about to happen, you start to panic and try to wriggle out of the way as the figure bends down beside Dr Addison. But rather than haul the academic to her feet and drag her away, the stranger sets to loosening the knots binding her. When Dr Addison is free, they turn their attention to helping you.

As soon as you are both free you hear a voice hiss, "Come on, this way!"

You are disoriented enough that you're unsure if it was the stranger or Dr Addison who spoke. Certainly, the feminine voice sounded familiar, but you thought it came from the door that now stands ajar, while the doctor is next to you.

But such uncertainties are irrelevant when it comes to fleeing your captors. Your savior ducks through the door and by the time you and Dr Addison have made it out of the room, you see them disappear around the corner at the end of the corridor you are in.

Muffled chanting fills the corridor from behind one of two other doors – the first to the left, the other to the right – but the reverberation of sound throughout the hall makes it difficult to determine which.

As you are considering which way to go in the poorly lit passageway, you can just make out curious murals covering the walls, although details are difficult to discern.

You have lost sight of your rescuer, but a soft voice carries from the end of the hall: "Don't delay – this way."

"We have to get out of here," Dr Addison urges you from behind, but your curiosity is piqued.

"Where are we?" you ask.

"I believe we have been captured by the Esoteric Order of Dagon," the academic replies. When you look at her blankly, she hurriedly explains. "They're a cult of fish-worshipping degenerates who practice human sacrifice to honor their blasphemous ocean-dwelling deities, which is why we have to get out of here now!"

You think the curious voices you can hear are coming from the door to the right, while golden light is spilling from the room to the left.

So, what do you want to do?

Go through the door to the left: turn to **278**.
Go through the door to the right: turn to **173**.
Follow your mysterious savior and head for the end of the corridor: turn to **193**.

Not knowing what else to do, you make your way back to the Gilman House Hotel on the off chance that Dr Addison might yet turn up there. Walking straight past the hotel manager, who is still on duty at the reception desk, you climb the stairs to Room #428. Perhaps there is some vital piece of information, most likely among the academic's research notes, that you missed the last time you were here.

Turn to **111**.

It is some months later when you are stunned to see Dr Addison again.

In the intervening weeks, you had almost managed to convince yourself that what happened on that day in Innsmouth had all been some dark dream, or a false memory born of a life-threatening fever. But while the outward marks of your ordeal have healed, visions of the horrors you witnessed in that corrupted place have haunted your dreams every night since.

You did not expect to see the academic ever again, but you are particularly surprised to see her looking so well. You were sure she was a goner that night after she entered the water. And you certainly weren't in any position to save her.

But as you regard her from the other side of the street, you do not feel inclined to make your presence known or speak with her. There is something unsettling about her manner, not in the same way that those afflicted with the "Innsmouth look" appeared unsettling, but as if she hasn't been put together right.

As you watch the fronds of her bright red hair rippling in the breeze, you are put in mind of sea stars that dwell in the ocean's depths, anchored by myriad tubular feet to the rocky outcroppings of hydrothermal vents while their free arms waft in the warm water, searching for food.

You feel a shiver of inexplicable, primordial fear pass through you and, turning on your heel, walk away. You have no desire to ever have anything to do with Dr Stella Addison again. After all, as they say, there are plenty more fish in the sea.

The End.

SECRETS CHECKLIST

As you find these SECRETS in play, check them off the list!

- ☐ *A Kettle of Fish*
- ☐ *Aqua Vitae*
- ☐ *Banged Up*
- ☐ *Between the Devil and the Deep Blue Sea*
- ☐ *Buried Treasure*
- ☐ *Catch of the Day*
- ☐ *Davy Jones's Locker*
- ☐ *Dead Men Tell No Tales*
- ☐ *Dead Signal*
- ☐ *Deep Regrets*
- ☐ *Deep Rising*
- ☐ *Dr Addison, I Presume*
- ☐ *Drunk and Disorderly*
- ☐ *Dutch Courage*
- ☐ *Father Dagon*
- ☐ *Fish Food*
- ☐ *Fish Supper*
- ☐ *Full Fathom Five*
- ☐ *Ghost Town*
- ☐ *Gone Fishing*
- ☐ *Hail Hydra*
- ☐ *Hidden One*
- ☐ *Hidden Two*
- ☐ *Hidden Three*
- ☐ *Hidden Four*
- ☐ *Hidden Five*
- ☐ *Hidden Six*
- ☐ *Hidden Seven*
- ☐ *I Do Like to be Beside the Seaside*
- ☐ *In Deep Water*
- ☐ *Lord Dagon*
- ☐ *Lost at Sea*
- ☐ *Odd Fish*
- ☐ *Old Sea Dogs' Tales*
- ☐ *Panic Attack*
- ☐ *Red Herring One*
- ☐ *Red Herring Two*
- ☐ *Red Herring Three*
- ☐ *Red Herring Four*
- ☐ *Red Herring Five*
- ☐ *Red Herring Six*
- ☐ *Red Herring Seven*
- ☐ *Secrets of the Sea*
- ☐ *Slippery as an Eel*
- ☐ *Something Fishy*
- ☐ *Spadework*
- ☐ *Swimming With the Fishes*
- ☐ *The Hungry Sea*
- ☐ *The Lighthouse*
- ☐ *The Shadow Over Innsmouth*
- ☐ *The Supreme Sacrifice*
- ☐ *The Yellow Wallpaper*
- ☐ *Wish You Were Here?*
- ☐ *With All Hands*
- ☐ *X Marks the Spot*

Super-Secrets Checklist

☐ Finish with a combined **COMBAT** + **INTELLECT** + **WILLPOWER** of 15 or more: *Hero.*

☐ Finish with at least three stars and a combined **COMBAT** + **INTELLECT** + **WILLPOWER** of 5 or less: *A Close Shave.*

☐ Finish with 2, 1 or 0 stars: *The Calamari's Revenge.*

☐ Finish the adventure using three different Investigators: *Saviors of Innsmouth.*

☐ Finish with *Dead Men Tell No Tales* + *Old Sea Dogs' Tales*: *The Song of the Sea.*

☐ Finish with *A Kettle of Fish* + *Gone Fishing* + *Something Fishy* + *Swimming With the Fishes*: *Plenty More Fish in the Sea.*

☐ Finish with a **SANITY** of 5 or more: *Sane.*

☐ Finish with a **HEALTH** of 5 or more: *In Rude Health.*

☐ Finish with a **DOOM** of 5 or more: *Doomed.*

☐ Finish with **10** or more **CLUES**: *The Seeker.*

☐ Finish with 5 or more **RESOURCES**: *Ready For Anything.*

☐ Finish with 0 **CLUES**: *Lucky.*

☐ Finish with 0 **RESOURCES**: *Empty-Handed.*

☐ Finish with a **HEALTH** of 0 or below: *Green Around the Gills.*

☐ Finish with a **SANITY** of 0 or below: *You Can't Handle the Truth!*

☐ Finish with a **SANITY** of 0 or below, a **HEALTH** of 0 or below, and you collect all 3 Weaknesses that can be gained in the game: *A High Price to Pay.*

- ☐ Finish without cheating even once: *Virtuous.*
- ☐ Battle 4 different types of opponents: *The Spawn of Innsmouth.*
- ☐ Find *Between the Devil and the Deep Blue Sea* + *Deep Rising* + *Father Dagon* + *Lord Dagon* across several playthroughs: *Bigger Fish to Fry.*
- ☐ Find *Aqua Vitae* + *Dr Addison, I Presume* + *Dutch Courage* + *Gone Fishing* + *Hail Hydra* + *Panic Attack* across several playthroughs: *Tunnel Vision.*
- ☐ Find the [CROWBAR], [HAMMER], and [SCREWDRIVER] across several playthroughs: *Toolbox.*
- ☐ Finish with the [WHISKEY] and the [MOONSHINE]: *Teetotal.*
- ☐ Find the [WHISKEY] and the [MOONSHINE] in one playthrough but finish with neither: *Drink Like a Fish.*
- ☐ Finish with [OCTOPUS CROWN] and [SEA GOLD]: *All that Glisters.*
- ☐ Finish with the [BOOK OF TIDE TIMES], [TREASURE HUNTER'S CHART], and [MAP OF THE TUNNELS]: *Local Knowledge.*
- ☐ Discover all new 27 items across various playthroughs: *Hoarder.*
- ☐ Discover all 14 unstarred endings: *Hapless.*
- ☐ Discover all 7 *Red Herring Secrets*: *Wild Goose Chase.*
- ☐ Discover all 7 *Hidden Secrets*: *Hunter.*
- ☐ Discover all 5 starred endings: *The Stars Align.*
- ☐ Collect all 31 ***Super-Secrets*** above this one: *Meticulous.*
- ☐ Collect all 54 in-text *Secrets*: *Tenacious.*
- ☐ And if you collect both ***Meticulous*** and ***Tenacious,*** award yourself *The End-of-the-Pier Show.*

Continuing the Adventure

If you're reading this, you have discovered that this book is part of the Investigators Gamebooks series. Once you've successfully completed any other gamebook in the series you can, if you wish, continue in a new adventure, such as this one, using your chosen Investigator. There is, of course, nothing to stop you starting fresh with a different Investigator, if you prefer.

If you do decide to continue with the same Investigator, they may gain **EXPERIENCE**, based on how you fared in adventures so far. After completing an adventure, or before beginning the next one, work through the following steps to keep your Investigator up to date.

EXPERIENCE: SKILLS, HEALTH, SANITY, AND DOOM

When you complete an adventure, your Investigator's **SKILLS**, **HEALTH**, **SANITY**, **RESOURCES**, **CLUES** and **DOOM** return to their original starting values. However, roll one die for each star you earned in completing the previous adventure. In each adventure, you can earn up to four stars.

For each die which rolls a 6, you may choose one of the following:

- Increase one of your skills (**WILLPOWER**, **INTELLECT** or **COMBAT**) by **+1** permanently. If any of your skills increased temporarily during the previous adventure, you should choose the skill which increased the most (if possible). Otherwise, it is your choice.
- Increase your starting **HEALTH** or **SANITY** by **+1**.
- Remove **1** starting **DOOM** from your Character Sheet.

For each die which rolls a 1, you must choose one of the following:

- Reduce one of your skills (**WILLPOWER**, **INTELLECT** or **COMBAT**) by -1 permanently. If any of your skills decreased temporarily during the previous adventure, you should choose the skill which decreased the most (if possible). Otherwise, it is your choice.
- Reduce your starting **HEALTH** or **SANITY** by -1.
- Add *1* starting **DOOM** to your Character Sheet.
- No skill may ever increase or decrease by more than +2/-2 from your Investigator's original starting value, and no skill may decrease to lower than 1.

Health and Sanity may not increase to more than 10 and may not be reduced to less than 1.

EXPERIENCE: ABILITIES AND WEAKNESSES

When you complete an adventure, you may choose one {**ABILITY**} gained during the adventure to add to your character sheet permanently. However, if you do so, you must also choose one {**WEAKNESS**} acquired during the adventure and add that to your Character Sheet permanently as well.

EXPERIENCE: ITEMS

When you complete an adventure, you may choose one [ITEM] gained during the adventure and add it to your character sheet. Other items are lost (although it's always possible you might come across the same or a similar item again in the future…). Simply put, there's only so much stuff you can carry.

RESOURCES AND CLUES

Experience does not affect **RESOURCES** or **CLUES**. Any **RESOURCES** or **CLUES** gained during the last adventure which you did not spend are lost.

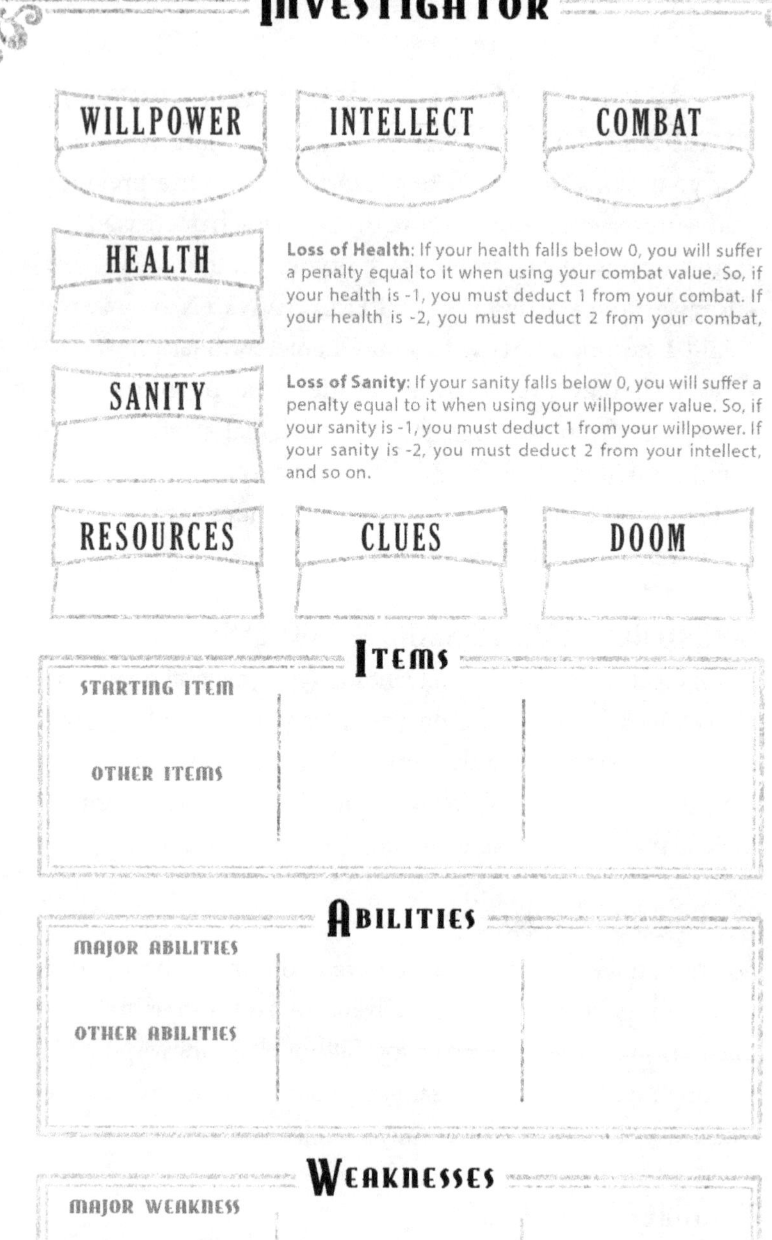

Investigator

WILLPOWER

INTELLECT

COMBAT

HEALTH

Loss of Health: If your health falls below 0, you will suffer a penalty equal to it when using your combat value. So, if your health is -1, you must deduct 1 from your combat. If your health is -2, you must deduct 2 from your combat,

SANITY

Loss of Sanity: If your sanity falls below 0, you will suffer a penalty equal to it when using your willpower value. So, if your sanity is -1, you must deduct 1 from your willpower. If your sanity is -2, you must deduct 2 from your intellect, and so on.

RESOURCES

CLUES

DOOM

Items

STARTING ITEM

OTHER ITEMS

Abilities

MAJOR ABILITIES

OTHER ABILITIES

Weaknesses

MAJOR WEAKNESS

OTHER WEAKNESSES

Acknowledgments

Innsmouth has long been a place I have wanted to visit, although it's not somewhere I would like to stay for very long. For my recent sojourn to the seaside, I have been joined by others who have dared to venture away from Arkham for a spot of fishing, people without whom this book would not be what it is. And so, I would like to thank Gwendolyn Nix and Matt Keefe at Aconyte Books, the franchise development team and Fantasy Flight Games, and Victor Cheng for his meticulous playtesting.

About the Author

Jonathan Green is an award-winning writer of speculative fiction, with more than eighty books to his name. He has written everything from *Fighting Fantasy* gamebooks to *Doctor Who* novels, by way of *Sonic the Hedgehog, Star Wars: The Clone Wars, Teenage Mutant Ninja Turtles,* and *Judge Dredd.* He is the creator of the Pax Britannia steampunk series for Abaddon Books, and the author of the critically-acclaimed, *YOU ARE THE HERO – A History of Fighting Fantasy Gamebooks.* For Aconyte Books, he is the author of *Arkham Horror Investigators Gamebooks: The Darkness Over Arkham.* He is currently writing his own ACE Gamebooks, which reimagine literary classics as interactive adventures.

www.ingramcontent.com/pod-product-compliance
Lightning Source LLC
Chambersburg PA
CBHW032003060525
26217CB00008B/51

* 9 7 8 1 8 3 9 0 8 3 3 5 8 *